SISTERSHIPS

A Fictional Tale Aboard Titanic's
Forgotten Sister the Olympic

To Robyn + Emrys,

all the best,

Elaine Gallagher

ELAINE GALLAGHER

Library and Archives Canada Cataloguing in Publication
 Gallagher, Elaine, author
     Sisterships : a fictional tale aboard Titanic's sister the
Olympic / Elaine Gallagher.
Includes bibliographical references.
Issued in print and electronic formats.

ISBN 978-1-77302-543-8 (hardcover).
ISBN 978-1-77302-542-1 (softcover).
ISBN 978-1-77302-544-5 (HTML).

I. Title.
PS8613.A45934S57 2017   C813'.6   C 2017-902369-1
                                          C2017-902370-5

DEDICATION

This book is dedicated to the memory
of my Grandmother Betsy Brown.

This book celebrates *Titanic's* sister ship, the *Olympic*.
The tragic Titanic saga often usurps Olympics' place
in history. And yet both ships were built side-by-
side, and were identical in almost every way.

TABLE OF CONTENTS

PREFACE

My maternal grandmother, Betsy Brown (nee Oakes)—the heroine of this story—provided the first inspiration for the book when in 1960, just before she died, she gave me a postcard with an X marked on a house in a village somewhere in England. "That was my birthplace and where I grew up," she claimed. After careful sleuthing I eventually located her village and have been privileged to visit there several times. I walked on her street. I felt at home somehow.

The wrinkled remains of Betsy's only record of her birthplace.

Betsy came to Canada in 1912 and sadly, never once returned to her beloved England. I spent many days of my youth prying stories from her about what life was like as she grew up, stories that appear in this book. One of the most fascinating of Grandma's stories was her claim that she had booked passage on the great ocean liner *Titanic*, but for some strange reason was reassigned to travel on the sister ship – the Olympic. I used to sit on her bed staring at the pictures of the two ships—the *Titanic* and her sister the *Olympic*—hanging on the wall at the head of her bed. Reminders, she would say, that you should never complain when things don't appear to go your way.

I spent the intervening years conducting research and collecting stories from others that would help me to understand what life was like back in the late 1800s and early 1900s in England. My travels took me into the British Maritime Museum at Greenwich, where I found information on the great ships of the White Star Line.

The townsfolk of Swadlincote also embraced me. Graham Nutt opened up the Magic Attic on a bank holiday so I could pore over old records and news-papers. There I saw the original slide projector and glass slides that were used to advertise Canada back at the turn of the last century. People gave me book-lets of stories about real events that comprise the history of this wonderful little corner of England.

They took me to the post office, where I was given old photographs of the town.

My research for this book has also put me in touch with the many fascinating accounts in print and online concerning the *Titanic* and her sinking. While I tried to incorporate many of the interesting facts that I unearthed, I kept reminding myself that this is a novel and I have taken some liberties blending fact with fiction for that period in time.

Rosa Molson – the stewardess in my story - was not a real person and while I drew from a biography of a stewardess named Violet Jessop for some of the background material about life as a ship stewardess on the *Titanic*, in particular what it was like to have been rescued from the sinking *Titanic*, this character is pure fiction. Most of the remaining characters in the book are fictional. The only people who retain their real names are Betsy Oakes and her family and closest associates.

I am indebted to my partner John for his patience and support. Stephen and Shannon, thanks for believing in me, even when I was not too sure of the road I was taking along this great journey. And a special thanks to Marg Gilks for her great editorial suggestions. In addition, I thank my Aunt Muriel Hilton, Betsy's only living child, for the original oil paintings of the Olympic and Titanic that appear on the cover.

CHAPTER ONE:
SETTING SAIL

May 17, 1912

The half-eaten scone sat before her as if daring her to take just one more bite. She was tempted. Lunch would be a long time coming. Betsy had spent half the night in the boarding house bathroom with an upset stomach. Enough was enough. She gingerly sipped her tea instead, gazing around at the other guests seated in the small, dark dining room of the Wayward Arms in Southampton, as she waited to be summoned to the carriage outside. She found it hard to believe the incredible events that had led her to this moment.

Betsy breathed a small sigh of relief when, minutes later, her father, Walter Oakes, appeared through the large panelled door and waved for her to come along outdoors. She followed him outside to the carriage where her trunk was safely loaded on the back.

Walter gave Betsy a hand up to climb into the middle passenger seat, and then followed her up.

The streets were still dark. A light rain fell, accentuating the clip-clop of the horse's hooves on the cobblestones. Betsy gripped her handbag nervously. Her heart hammered with excitement.

The carriage rounded a corner, and there it was. A ship, grander than anything she could have imagined, and far more spectacular than the ads and posters had depicted it.

A vintage postcard from the Olympic

Betsy tipped her head back, her eyes following the four magnificent smokestacks that rose towering into the air. And there, high on the mast, was the red flag bearing the unmistakable White Star logo. Her breath caught in her throat. "Oh Father, it's unbelievable!" she exclaimed. She lowered her gaze to the man seated next to her. "Oh, how I wish you were coming with me!"

Walter's face was a canvas of mixed emotions, He wordlessly placed his arm around his daughter's shoulders and squeezed tightly.

The carriage came to a halt at the end of a long line of carts and vehicles dropping off their passengers. They climbed out and Watty, the name Walter's mates had assigned to him, paid the driver, who then transferred her large trunk from their carriage to the baggage handler on the dock. "Have a wonderful trip," the driver called back as he drove off.

Tears welled up in Betsy's eyes. "I know you want the best for me, but it's all so frightening—leaving England, leaving you. And travelling on that ship!" Her gaze strayed back to the behemoth waiting in its berth. She looked back to her father. "Maybe I made the wrong decision. Maybe I shouldn't do it. I worry for you. And the ship...Oh Dad what am I doing?"

"Oh, Betsy, I'm going to be just fine, my dearest. I've told you over and over, I'm too old to make a trip like that across that vast ocean. I want you to go to Canada and make a wonderful new life for yourself. Your new employer is waiting for you to arrive. And the ship, well...they tell us its perfectly safe now. I wouldn't let you sail on it if I didn't think that was true."

Slowly they walked to the bottom of the ship's loading ramp. "Sweetheart, it's going to be a real adventure," Watty continued. "You can write to me every day and tell me all about it. I'll get to live it with you through your letters."

Blinking back tears, Betsy nodded, and then gave him a goodbye hug and, tightly gripping the small suitcase that contained her travelling clothes, she turned to start up the long ramp to the ship's main entranceway. She fell in line with other excited passengers making their way on board, eyes scanning the deck above her. Seeing the captain standing with the first mate and several other crewmembers, greeting the guests one by one as they stepped aboard, Betsy ran one hand down the skirt of her long brown dress to smooth it, her other hand straying to touch the hand-tatted white lace collar she wore at her neck.

As she waited her turn, she looked around. So many pieces of luggage accompanied the first class ladies! Probably the result of weeks spent shopping in the high fashion houses of London and Paris, she decided, eyeing their maids, servants, and even a few pet dogs tucked under their arms. One woman carried a bird in its cage.

Betsy approached an officer, who then asked her name. The officer then read out her entry in the ship manifest: "*Oakes, Betsy. Twenty-eight-year-old female; single; servant, seamstress; can read/write; English race; last permanent residence England, Swadlincote, Derbyshire. Relative from whence she came: father—Mr.*

Walter Oakes, 35 Alma Road, Newhall, England. Final destination: Craven, Saskatchewan, Canada. Paid by self: $50. In Canada before: no. In prison: no. Polygamist: no. Anarchist: no. Promise of labour: yes. Health: good; deformed/crippled: no; five feet tall, fair complexion, brown hair, blue eyes, no marks. Born: England, Swadlincote." He looked up. "Did we get all that correct, Miss Oakes?"

Betsy smiled and nodded.

At the end of the long line of captain, crew and stewards, a beautiful young woman about Betsy's age extended her hand and introduced herself in a voice with a faint Italian accent. "Welcome on board, Miss Oakes. I am Rosa Molson, one of the ship stewardesses. I will be serving your section of the ship on this voyage."

The woman was about an inch taller than Betsy, who was struck by her intense green eyes, shiny black hair, and full, sensuous lips. The traditional stewardess uniform that she wore—a soft blue dress and starched white sleeves, collar, and apron bearing a large red cross—accentuated her tiny waist. Her shoes and stockings were also white. A small, stiff white cap adorned her head.

There was something about Rosa's deportment that struck Betsy as sad. Perhaps it was the slight stoop of her shoulders, or maybe the downcast eyes. When she shook the woman's hand, it felt clammy. She couldn't explain why, but Betsy felt drawn to this woman and vowed to get to know her better if she had the opportunity. There was something mysterious about her.

"Oh, thank you so much," Betsy replied. "I have never so much as set foot on a ship before, so I don't know how I'll feel if the voyage is at all rough."

Rosa nodded. "It can certainly get nasty out in the ocean at times. It may comfort you to know that this ship was built to be particularly stable in rough seas. And of course even more improvements have been made on her, since her sister's tragic accident. I personally have made a number of crossings and found her to be better than any ship built to date. I will check in with you later tonight to see how you are managing. You are to let me know if there is anything I can do to make your voyage more enjoyable."

"I really look forward to seeing you later," Betsy said, and moved on. She had more than seasickness on her mind. It had only been one month since this ship's sister—the great *Titanic*—had crashed into an iceberg in the Atlantic and sunk with many of her passengers still on board. She wanted to ask more questions about the improvements that had been made on the *Olympic*. It was clear Rosa knew more than what she was revealing in their brief encounter.

Betsy moved to the railing to search the dock for a last wave to her father. She spotted her father's stooped frame on the wharf, and caught his eye. Then she waved goodbye and threw down a streamer for him to catch, a kind of token last handshake that had become customary for those emigrating, as a final farewell to their relatives, friends and their homeland. Then with the orchestra on shore playing *"Will ye no come back again"* in the background, the ship set sail. *How odd,* she thought. *I could swear he's weeping.* All along, he had put up a strong front, never once faltering in his encouragement for her to head off to the new world. *I wonder whether I misjudged his enthusiasm over my departure.*

When she thought back, she remembered him telling her of rumours of unrest developing in Europe, unrest that, some people said, if unchecked, could lead to a great war among European nations. "If that happens," she remembered him saying, "I'll take comfort that my last surviving daughter is far away in a land that is not embroiled in the conflicts." He'd kept telling her how brave she was, to be setting off on this journey alone to a land she'd never seen. But somehow she didn't feel at all brave at this moment. In fact, she was terrified.

With the final blast of the ship's whistle, Betsy stared off into the distance. *Just how safe is this ship?* she wondered for the umpteenth time. And as the ship slowly moved away from the dock, she thought back to that day in Woodville when her family gathered for a group photo, the last one to be taken before her sister and mother died, only a year apart.

And she reflected back over the series of unexpected events that had led up to her being here.

The last family photo of the Oakes Family circa 1904.

CHAPTER TWO:
WHEN ONE DOOR CLOSES

Betsy stood at the railing and breathed deeply. She reflected back to the day ten years ago when it had all started out so innocently. At age eighteen, she had answered the ad in the *Burton Post* for a housemaid position in nearby Birmingham.

She recalled arriving at the Turnball's on a gloriously sunny June morning and being greeted by a young woman in a maid's uniform. "Come in, come in," she'd urged, waving Betsy forward. "You must be the new help. You do know the Missus is in a state of advanced pregnancy. The babe is due in a few week's time and Mrs. Turnball has been confined to bed for a month because of premature leakage of fluid. I've quit and am leaving tomorrow. You'll be caring for the new infant soon I suspect."

Betsy had been taken aback; the ad had only asked for someone to serve as a domestic. She was even more surprised when, two weeks later, the woman went into full labour. Then, immediately after returning from the local infirmary, Mrs. Turnball thrust the newborn baby, Margery, into Betsy's arms and said, "I did all I am going to do. You look after her now." With that she retreated into her room, where she remained for weeks and then months. The doctors declared her in a state of severe post-partum depression.

Betsy's experience from helping neighbours with younger children had provided her with some of the basics of childcare, but she was even more grateful for the advice of the nannies who frequented the nearby park with their little ones in tow.

But if she was somewhat ill prepared for nanny service, she had been even less prepared for the affection the master of the house began to bestow upon her. The longer his wife barricaded herself away from the family, the lonelier he became, and soon Betsy found herself sitting by his side next to the fireplace night after night, once the wee one was secure in her cradle. She smiled now as she recalled the first night he told her how beautiful she was.

Betsy, a virgin, was afraid, and knew this was wrong, but the intimacy, and desire, grew too great and in time, the two became lovers. She shivered as she remembered how he convinced her that she filled a huge void in his life and while he could never marry her, he would make sure she was cared for while in their service. Of course they had to be discreet.

There were other servants in the home and while his wife spent most of her time in her room, there was always the chance she would appear at an awkward moment. Charles would often creep into Betsy' room in the middle of the night and while she thrilled to his touch during those dark hours, she found it hard to get up in the early morning to attend to the growing toddler's needs and wants.

Days had drifted into months and then years. On many days Betsy fantasized that she was the mistress of the house, and that young Margery belonged to her and the master. Margery flourished under her devotion and together they spent long, wonderful hours exploring the parks and trails in the nearby township.

Betsy and her young niece

Betsy tried to recall an exact event or day when she began to question her happiness in the Turnball household. *Perhaps it began in the park when I watched couples walking about arm in arm, pushing a pram on a warm spring day. Or maybe it was when my best friend, Ruth Collins, who had immigrated to Canada, wrote and said she was about to be married to a wonderful man.* The feelings of discontent had grown until one day she woke up knowing that life as she knew it could not continue. If she didn't leave the Turnball's she might never have a chance for a home of her own, a man of her own—*And most importantly, a child of my own,* she thought. *I am twenty-eight and life is passing me by. It may already be too late.*

That very day she approached Charles in the hallway as he returned from work. Making sure no one was nearby, she put her hand on his arm and said in a low voice, "I must speak to you in private, Charles."

He frowned, noticing the strain on her face, and said, "Alright. I will quickly change and meet you in the library."

Betsy went immediately to the small, book-lined room, glad for the fire burning in the hearth; she was shivering—though with a chill or nerves, she wasn't sure. Restive, she roamed the room, absently caressing the books lying on the desk before sitting on the edge of one of the chairs facing the great oak desk. *Am doing the right thing?* she pondered. *My life here has been wonderful in certain ways. I have come to love Margery and her father so much. But they aren't mine to love. It's like I have borrowed them.* She looked around the room. *Like books from a library. I have to return them to their rightful owner.* She nodded, her decision made.

Betsy rose quickly when Charles stepped into room. He pulled the door shut behind him, the smile he gave Betsy tentative. "Betsy?"

"Charles." Betsy stopped, gathering her scattered thoughts. *It's the right thing,* she reminded herself. "I'm not sure where to begin, Charles, but I have made an important decision." She swallowed, watching him. "Perhaps the most important decision of my life."

He'd been approaching, but now he stopped, eyebrows lifted in concern. "Why Betsy, whatever have you decided?"

She clasped her hands together to prevent herself from wringing them. "Charles, I am going to resign my position here. I can no longer put off trying to have a life of my own. I don't know if you can mend things with your wife. But my being here isn't helping you in that regard. It's only a matter of time until she discovers our affair. It's best I go now. For everyone."

She could see that Charles was in shock. His mouth gaped open, then closed and opened again as he struggled for something to say, words that would make her change her mind. Then he closed his mouth and his expression softened. He nodded. In his heart, Charles knew he had to let her go. He had always known one day it would be so. Betsy bit her lip, both relieved and saddened. It was over. Her life was about to change, and she had no idea where it would go from here.

* * *

The following morning, Betsy remembered approaching the mistress of the house and telling her of her decision to leave. "Are you sure about this?" asked Mrs. Turnball.

Betsy had had time to think the night before, and she was confident she had made the right decision. "Yes, I am very sure," she said. "I think it is best for everyone if I start a life of my own, away from here."

Strangely, Mrs. Turnball offered not one word of resistance. In fact, she suggested that Betsy be prepared to depart the following day. *Does she suspect?* This would be an easy solution for Mrs. Turnball, if she did. *In which case, she won't want me to have a change of heart,* Betsy thought wryly.

There was a sombre hush throughout the house when, later that afternoon, Mrs. Turnball invited Betsy to have tea with her. Betsy felt as though the silence was a forewarning of ominous events about to unfold, and she hesitated before entering the drawing room where the older woman waited, seated in one of the velvet wingback chairs before the hearth. Phipps, the large grey housecat, drowsed with heavy-lidded violet eyes on a soft cushion beside the hearth, and a white cloth had been draped on the leather-covered tea table between Mrs. Turnball's chair and the one she gestured for Betsy to take. The heavy drapes covering the floor-to-ceiling windows had been pulled aside, and sun streamed in from the English garden, its colours muted by winter's grip.

Betsy sat stiffly in the armchair and waited as the housemaid served tea. Annie Turnball waited silently, her hair pulled back in its usual harsh coif and her plain black dress making her look years older than forty-three.

As the maid left, ten-year-old Margery skipped merrily into the room, then wilted immediately after one glance at her mother's face, knowing she had been summoned for some serious reason. Betsy would normally have smiled, certain that Margery feared she'd been found out for some misbehaviour. The youngster so often left her muddy shoes in the hallway, or was caught sneaking extra biscuits from the tray at tea.

"Sit down here Margery," said her mother, pointing to the footstool by her feet. Her face was drawn, her expression stern, but her hand returned to accompany the other in wrestling with a dainty lace handkerchief in her lap, belying her composure. "I have some terrible news...

Margery's eyes grew wide. "Tell me, tell me!" she implored, near tears. She was shaken by her mother's intensity, so seldom seen in the face of her long-standing depression and the complacency instilled by years of privilege. Her father had managed to get very rich from investing in a small factory that made steel pipes, and they had hired Betsy to help raise their one and only child right.

"Well, the news is that Miss Betsy here," she glanced at Betsy, "our trusty maid, is going to be leaving us. She has decided to move back home to Swadlincote."

Margery turned huge eyes on Betsy. "Oh, Betsy!" she cried. "Why would you leave me? I have always had you with me. You simply can't go and leave me here." She whirled to face her mother in anger. "Mommy, why would you let her go?"

"I believe she wishes to be with her ailing father. She will be leaving in the morning. I'm sorry I didn't have more time to warn you." Mrs. Turnball sighed at Margery's stricken expression. "I know how fond you are of her, and no wonder—she's been with you since you were a baby. But she has to leave."

Margery burst into tears. Betsy fought back tears of her own. Margery was even closer to Betsy than to her own mother. This was devastating news for the young lass. Mrs. Turnball gathered Margery into her arms and nodded at Betsy to dismiss her. Betsy rose and moved quickly to the door.

Betsy heard the quick footsteps and breathless sobs behind her as she climbed the staircase to her room—Margery had followed her. *Oh Margery, poor dear, I'm so sorry,* she thought, bracing herself for what was to come. Betsy knew the little girl's mind would be racing with reasons she would use to implore her to stay, and probably even more reasons to take her with her. The strain between her parents in recent years had made the home a tense place to be—except when she could escape to the playroom or head out somewhere on an adventure with Miss Betsy.

They entered Betsy's room and Margery fell crying onto the bed when she saw that Betsy had already packed most of her things into a large worn trunk. Tears came flooding out, dampening the chequered pillowcase. Betsy sat down beside her and placed her arm over her shoulder. "Margery, darling, I wouldn't leave you if I didn't have to. You must be a brave young girl and learn to carry on here on your own. Next year you will be off to boarding school and we would have been apart regardless. I will miss you, and I shall write. You will be in my heart forever. In fact I promise to name my firstborn daughter after you if the good Lord should bless me with a baby girl. I love you so dearly my pet."

Margery turned over and flung her arms around Betsy's neck. "I will never forget you either, Miss Betsy," she sobbed. "I love you too. I just can't bear the idea of never seeing you again. You mustn't go and leave me. If you have to go, take me with you. I beg you."

"Darling, I have to go. It has nothing to do with you; I have my own reasons for leaving. If I had my way, I'd pack you up and take you along. You will be fine. Maybe you'll get to know your mother better, with me gone. She cares about you deeply, you know."

Betsy spent a few more minutes soothing the young girl, then gently took her hand and led her to her own room to prepare for bed. Margery said her prayers and then Betsy tucked her into bed just as she had for the past ten years. Finally the sobbing eased and the young girl slowly drifted into an uneasy sleep. Betsy wiped barely contained tears from her own eyes as she returned to her own room.

That night, Betsy tried desperately to fall asleep, but sleep would not come. She lay in bed, half awake, her mind churning as she contemplated her future. When early morning sunlight began creeping through the curtains of her tiny bedroom window, she rose and dressed for the long journey home, still uncertain about what the future held for her.

* * *

Betsy and 10 year-old Margery

Wrapped in a dark, floor-length cloak with a black fur collar against the cold, Betsy sat next to Charles in the buggy as they headed for the train station. Neither spoke at first, and the only sound was the thud of the horse's hooves and the creak and rumble of the carriage over the rough roads. Finally he turned to her, and Betsy was surprised to see tears glistening in his eyes. "I will miss you terribly, Betsy," he said softly. "You have been the light of my life for the past ten years. I saw the wisdom in you—wisdom beyond your years, and a warm heart that would nurture our growing daughter. I don't know how Margery will survive without you." He caught his breath and paused. With a lump in his throat he whispered, "I don't know how I will survive."

Betsy was quiet. She fought back tears as the realization struck: she would never see his dear face again. She reached for his trembling hand and held it to her face. "Charles," she said, "I will never forget you. I am so grateful for all the kindness you have shown me. I will miss you terribly. But it's for the best that I leave."

The carriage arrived at the train station in Birmingham and Charles alighted first, and then offered his hand to help her descend. He kept her hand in his and pulled her into one last embrace, tight with the finality of goodbye. They parted as the porter marched away with her suitcase, tears streaming down their cheeks, hands still clasped. Finally Betsy turned away and climbed on board the train, finding a window seat so she could see the platform.

"Who am I?" she whispered as tears rolled down her flushed cheeks. "Whatever happened to the feisty, adventurous teenager that left home ten years ago? I feel like I'm on a slippery mountainside with nothing to grasp."

Betsy brooded on what lay ahead for her as the train left the station, and didn't focus on what was passing by the window until the train was weaving its way across the Midlands, with the smokestacks for the pottery kilns and the dark openings of mines that dotted the countryside. But partway through her journey she began to feel a new emotion creeping in. It was a vague sense of excitement over the possibilities. Maybe, just maybe, there was a man out there somewhere who would appreciate her true worth as a woman even at her age, and would want to take her for his bride. *I'm going to try hard to turn this nasty affair into an opportunity,* she swore. *It's what my mother would have expected of me.*

CHAPTER THREE:
A ROAD LESS TRAVELLED

March 15, 2012

It was a one-hour carriage ride from Burton-on-Trent, where the train had stopped, to Swadlincote, or Swad as the locals called it. The area was made up of three separate settlements—Church Gresley, Newhall, and Swadlincote. *It's good to be home,* she thought, gazing fondly at the passing collieries, brickworks, and potteries as her carriage headed into town. Access to both rail and canal transportation made the region, already rich in raw materials, an appealing place to establish prosperous industry.

The short, square chimneys of potteries rose all around Swadlincote. The town's specialty was ceramic sinks and toilets, mostly plain white ones. The exception was Sharpe's Pottery, the kiln just off High Street. Sharpe's turned out bathroom fixtures of all kinds, beautifully decorated in delicate blue designs. It was rumoured that Queen Victoria herself had ordered all of her toilet fixtures from Sharpe's Pottery and from that of the nearby Thomas Crapper and Co. factory.

At the corner of Belmont and Church Streets her carriage passed by Belmont Primary School. "That's where my sister and I went to primary school," Betsy remarked to the driver. Then a flood of memories came over her. "I clearly remember the winter of

1886. It was a particularly cold January. The miners had gone without pay raises for several years and everyone was struggling to make ends meet. My parents finally decided that Mother should go to work. A box company in Woodhall hired her on. But then her problem was what to do with me, as I was only four and not in school yet."

"That's still a problem today for working mothers, isn't it?" commented the driver.

"Yes it is," replied Betsy, and suddenly brightened. "In fact, I've had an idea to set up a house where working mothers could drop their children off for the day. I think there would be quite a use for that sort of thing. Childcare isn't a problem for rich people. They have their nannies and governesses."

The driver nodded. "It's the working class that are penalized for having children—and just about everything else! It's a shame. So what did your parents do to handle their dilemma?"

Betsy sighed. "Mother searched high and low for an answer. In the end, the only solution was to send me to school with my sister, Sarah. She was two years older than me. I was very tiny for my age and very susceptible to the cold. I still am." As if to punctuate that statement, Betsy drew the cloak tighter around her shoulders. Then she smiled. "And I was still accustomed to having afternoon naps. So the teacher made up a bed for me in a drawer under the chalkboard. I took in a blanket and that's where I spent many long hours that winter."

The driver laughed. "Did you happen to learn any of the lessons being given by your sister's teacher?"

Betsy nodded. "Yes, as a matter of fact, I started reading before the end of that year. In a way it wasn't all that good, though, because when I started school for real I was very bored. I never could get excited about going to school after that."

"That's too bad," said the driver, "that it put you off of school." He tipped his chin to indicate the road ahead. "We're almost at your destination."

Moments later he turned the carriage onto Alma Road, the narrow street where Betsy had been born and raised. It was only one block long, with brick row houses on either side, their dark brown darkened further by the soot that blew from the smokestacks of the coal-fired pottery kilns in the area to settle on the buildings. Betsy was proud of her nondescript little road; it was one of the few remaining streets in all of England that was still owned by the people who lived there. They were strong believers in controlling their own neighbourhood, and when the county tried to take over, they staged a public protest and agitated so strongly, the mayor finally gave in.

The driver pulled the horses to a halt before number 35 and jumped nimbly down to off-load her trunk, then held his arm out for her as she stepped down. Betsy saw movement of curtains on either side of the street as curious neighbours peered through their windows at the new arrival. She compressed her lips in annoyance, wishing they would mind their own business. Already she dreaded the steady stream of nosy visitors who would drop by to satisfy their curiosity about the conditions of her return.

No twitching curtain in the window of her house; she'd telegraphed ahead to let her father know when she'd be arriving, and now fully expected to find her father sitting in the parlour, awaiting her arrival. With the driver waiting behind her with her trunk, she swung the door open, calling, "Father, I'm home." Her eyes instantly fell on her father, and she smiled and ran forward to embrace him.

Watty stood and opened his arms to welcome her. Betsy fell into them, and even the strong odour of stale beer and pipe tobacco failed to disturb her on this occasion. She thought she would cry with joy.

Slowly she withdrew from his arms and turned to tell the driver, "Up the stairs and first door on the left with that if you please, sir."

The man panted up the stairs, relieved himself of her trunk and Betsy thanked him, paid him, and sent him on his way. Then she turned back to her father, who led her into the small kitchen, saying, "I expect you're hungry after your journey; come along then; I've made a roast and some potatoes."

Betsy happily recounted her journey as Watty set out the dinner. The aroma of roast beef made her mouth water and she realized she had not eaten all day. "I'm famished!" she exclaimed, and her father grinned before turning back to the sink to drain the boiled potatoes.

Betsy moved to the window. Outside, in the distance, she could see the head of Mine 39, one of the many coalmines in the region, and the one where her father had toiled for nearly forty years. "Father, do you remember how much I used to love visiting the muscular little horses that were tied up at the mouth of the mine?" She paused to search her memory. "Jimmy and Nickel were my two favourites. They hauled up the heavy cartloads of coal from down below, didn't they?"

"Yes," Watty replied, nodding. "You admired their strength and devotion to the pit bosses. But you always felt sorry for them and brought them treats of oranges and carrots." Watty sighed. "It was sad, really. The coal dust blinded many of them eventually, but during their lifetime, the mine owners treated them very well." He chuckled wryly. "Folks said they were better fed and cared for than us miners, because they were part of the assets attached to the mine. We, on the other hand, were expendable."

Betsy glanced off to the left, where loomed the spire of St. John's Church, the place where she and most of the other Swadlincote children had been christened. It reminded her that she had not been to church for many months now. Maybe she would walk down that way in the morning after she was rested up, and see if the vicar was about.

She could just barely make out Oversetts Road and the entrances to the three inns clustered there—the Crown Inn, the Spread Eagle Inn, and the Oversetts Inn. She remembered many a night spent peering in the windows of each place until she located her father to summon him for supper. Rimed in coal dust and smelling heavily of ale, he would grasp her small hand in his and together they would make their way up to Alma Road.

Betsy remembered how her mother would be waiting at the door when they arrived home. Hands on hips and lips pursed, she would utter some words of welcome and note that the dinner was getting cold. Thoughts of her mother's recent death washed over her and she felt a great pang of sadness. It had only been two years. She had not yet recovered from her sister Sarah's tragic death from pneumonia when the good Lord sought to take away her mother.

She then recalled how her father would wash off as much coal dust as he could, slip out of his work clothes and don clean clothing to join his family at the table. He always said grace, and there were times when Betsy wondered how he could be grateful for the meagre bits of food that were assembled for the evening meal. This was especially true during the times the miners were on strike for months on end.

Her mother was amazingly creative, though, and they never did feel like they were starving.

Betsy smiled, remembering those days of yore. She turned to her father, now white-haired and stoop-shouldered, and asked if there was anything new going on in the village since her visit the previous summer.

"We have a new tram service running up High Street. It caused quite a bit of excitement the first day it started operating. And the Free Library on Alexandra Road has opened a lecture hall," he reported. "They are showing slides this week to advertise the wonders of Canada. The shipping lines have all contributed to the show, including the White Star Line. You have heard that they are launching their second great ocean liner—the *Titanic*—in April, have you not?"

Betsy nodded. Indeed, almost everyone in England had heard of the White Star Line's two new ships, the *Titanic* and the *Olympic*. They were to be the largest ocean-going vessels in the world. Built side by side in Belfast, the ships were said to be identical in almost every way. The first of the two to be completed, the *Olympic*, had had her maiden voyage already. The second was scheduled for launching in April, only two months hence. She wondered what it would be like to travel on a vessel so vast, going somewhere as far away as North America.

It wasn't the first time Betsy had considered what life might be like abroad. Only last week she had received another postcard from her old school chum, Ruth Collins, encouraging her to think about coming to Canada. Following the death of her mother four years before, Ruth had travelled with her father and brother to a small prairie town in Saskatchewan, where they had all found work with local farmers. Ruth had met and married a young Scotsman. As young women they had often wondered if they would both wind up being spinsters.

Ruth sent cards home to Betsy every couple of months and each time, she pleaded with her friend to consider joining her in the "land of promise." The latest card read:

January 1, 1912

Thinking of you, my dearest Betsy. Please give serious thought to joining me here. There are at least five men for every single woman. Many are hard-working farmers, honest, God-fearing gentlemen. I have already picked out several that you might like. If you need help with the fare, Roger and I would be happy to lend you the money until you get settled. I am sending some job advertisements in a separate envelope. You mustn't stay in that dreary place forever. You will simply wilt. It is cold here in winter, but almost always sunny.

Love, Ruth

"You know, Father, I have considered leaving England," she said as she moved away from the window and took the bowl of potatoes from him to set it on the table. "It would certainly be better than staying here and getting trapped in another position that offered no future and no opportunity for bettering my status in life." Looking about the humble kitchen, she recalled her many dreams of having her own freestanding home one day. "I dream of a place with fields all around, with room for a brood of youngsters to run and play."

Watty grunted and pursed his lips, making his bushy white moustache bristle. "So you'll be wanting to go to the lecture hall this week then."

Betsy pictured herself in a starched apron, busily cooking a massive meal for her husband and the farmhands. She imagined how wonderful the prairie air would smell without the soot and smog of the steel mills in Birmingham or the pottery kilns in Swadlincote. "Yes, I think so," she said. Canada certainly seemed a place where her dreams might materialize.

* * *

March 18, 1912

Betsy had to keep herself from walking too fast for her father to keep pace as they headed to the library to see the slide show and listen to the lecture about Canada. She had so many questions! Surely she'd get some answers tonight.

She felt her cheeks warm and her heart pick up its beat as they entered the crowded hall. The hum of many conversations as those waiting passed the time added to her sense of excitement. She smiled at her father and clasped his arm tighter for a moment. They found seats halfway down the hall and once settled, Betsy looked around. She recognized several of her old school chums and most of the neighbours from Alma Road. It wasn't a surprise to her that so many people were interested in seeking new opportunities abroad. Times were tough in Swadlincote, and many people were at risk of losing everything due to the lengthy strikes at the mine and the dwindling demand for porcelain bathroom fixtures. In fact, all over England, people were struggling to find work.

The lights dimmed and the hum of conversation fell off. A man dressed in a black jacket and waistcoat, gold watch chain glinting across his waist, crossed to the podium placed to the right of a large white screen and cleared his throat. "Ladies and gentlemen, welcome," he began, as the projectionist fussed with final preparations at a small table set a short distance away from the screen. He at last lit the projection machine's candle and nodded to the speaker, who in turn nodded to someone off in the shadows, and the room darkened completely.

A murmur of appreciation rose from the audience as the projectionist placed the first tinted glass slide into the gold-coloured machine—a breathtaking image of glorious mountains, a river, and tall green evergreens. The speaker smiled confidently and launched into his verbal documentary.

Betsy drew in a huge breath when that first image appeared, and when several others appeared, as well. Nothing in England bore any resemblance to this magnificent scenery. Produced by the Canadian Pacific Railroad, the show included scenes of virginal forests, open plains, rivers, Niagara Falls, fruit orchards, and the cities of Toronto and Montreal. The big appeal was for people who wanted land. They would be given very reasonably priced acreage as long as they agreed to build a house within the first year, the speaker assured them. "Canada wants settlers," he stated flatly. "Employment is assured. Married couples, women, household workers, boys and youths and single men are urgently needed."

As she listened to the speaker touting the wonders of Canada, a sense of calm come over Betsy. In those moments, in the darkened auditorium, she felt as if her destiny were unfolding before her eyes. The show ended with appealing ads from the White Star

Line and several other shipping lines. The speaker directed interested parties to Nixon's Shipping Office on Uxbridge Street in Burton-on-Trent, five kilometres from Swadlincote, for further particulars and ticket purchases. "They are the official agents for the Canadian Pacific Railway," the speaker added.

What caught Betsy's attention was the ad for the newest White Star ocean liner to be launched on April 10. She listened avidly as the speaker provided details about the *Titanic* and her sister ship, *Olympic*.

"In 1907, the Cunard Line, a rival of the White Star Line, launched two magnificent ships—the *Lusitania* and the *Mauretania*," he boomed, turning first to address the right side of the hall, then the left, as if uttering information of great portent. Then his voice settled into a storyteller's lilt. "These ships were luxurious and reliable, and as a result, the White Star Line was losing customers. So that year, Bruce Ismay, superintendent of the White Star Line, went to the house of Lord Perrie, a senior member of the shipbuilding firm of Harland and Wolff. It is reputed that over brandy and cigars, they gave birth to the idea of constructing three new ocean liners that would surpass anything currently on the seas in terms of size and luxury. These new vessels would be one hundred feet longer than the Cunard liners," his voice boomed out again, "and big enough to carry thirty-five hundred crew and passengers. The first two of these would be called the Olympic and the Titanic".

"Construction began on the *Olympic* on December 16, 1908, in Belfast. Next to her, in slip number three, work began on the *Titanic* on March 31, 1909. The ships are identical in almost every way. The original plans were for three funnels, but a fourth was added simply for show, and to serve as a ventilator. The only way one can tell the two ships apart is that on the *Olympic*, the promenade on A Deck is open its entire length, whereas on the *Titanic*, it is only open for half of its length. Large windows cover the other half."

"The interior of these two ships is unlike anything the world has seen on an ocean-going vessel. There are three lifts in first class and one in the very luxurious second class. Both first and second class are equipped with a spacious dining saloon, a library, and a barbershop. Also on board are squash courts, a steam room, the Veranda Café, an a la carte restaurant, and a swimming pool. The forward and aft grand stairways are magnificently hand carved out of the finest mahogany and polished to a fine gloss. There is even a telephone system on board."

"Can you believe all that? Imagine. A telephone on a ship!" Betsy whispered to her father. *Such luxuries, and on an ocean-going vessel! Some of the things the man described are rare, even on land,* she thought.

"The *Olympic* set sail on her maiden voyage on June 14, 1911. A flawless first voyage, I might add.

Her first crossing was accomplished in five days, sixteen hours, and forty-two minutes. Bruce Ismay travelled on board personally, to determine if any changes were needed. When The Olympic arrived in New York's harbour, her propeller was so powerful, the prop wash pulled in another ship—the *O.L. Hallenvach*—and caused serious damage to that ship's rudder and stern frame. The Olympic herself was undamaged."

The speaker grew sombre. "The ship was performing extremely well overall. However, on her fifth crossing, on September 20th, the Olympic was heading to Cherbourg, France to pick up passengers when she collided with *HMS Hawke* in the fog. The Olympic was left with a large gash on her starboard side and a damaged propeller, but fortunately no one was injured on board either ship. The ship was sent to Belfast to undergo repairs but sailed again on November 20th. On February 24th of this year, 1912, she shuddered and lost a propeller, and had to return to Belfast for more repairs."

He brightened. "She should be sailing in several days. Captain Edward Smith has steered the *Olympic* on all nine of her voyages, but he has been ordered to give up his position to Captain Herbert James Haddock in order to take over the helm of the *Titanic*. That ship is scheduled to launch on April 10th."

He finished his talk by announcing that there were still tickets available for this marvellous, once-in-a-lifetime opportunity to sail on the maiden voyage of a luxury liner—the *Titanic*.

Betsy could barely contain her excitement. She knew what she wanted to do, what direction her first steps on her new path to the future should be. "Oh Father," she declared, tucking her hand into his elbow as they left the hall and stepped out into the crisp night air, "Canada is more lovely than I ever imagined. I truly feel it's where my future lies. Why don't you sell the house here in Swadlincote and we'll go together to start a new life there. Then I would not have to feel guilty about leaving you."

Watty was walking slowly. He reached over and squeezed Betsy's hand. "I thank you for wanting to include me in your plans, but there are a host of reasons why I can't come with you. First, I am too old to work now, so there is a good chance I would not even qualify as an immigrant. I also don't think my health would stand the long voyage over there." He smiled at her and patted her hand. "Don't you worry about me. I am happy here. I have my friends."

"Well, if you won't consider coming with me, I could definitely send money home to help with your living costs," declared Betsy.

"Even that isn't necessary," claimed Watty. "Prime Minister Asquith just introduced the Old Age Pensions Act. Which means everyone with limited income over age seventy receives a regular pension now, and can live quite comfortably. People all over England are saying 'God bless Lloyd George,' you know."

Betsy nodded. She'd read about David Lloyd George, the Chancellor of the Exchequer, and his 1909 budget in the newspaper. It was designed to pay for these and all the other reforms he introduced, even if it did raise income tax.

"It came in at just the right time for me," Watty said. "So you see, I am best off here. While I will miss you, I want you to go and get on with your life."

Betsy smirked. "They also put new duties on tobacco and spirits, Father. What you gained in Old Age Pension money, you are spending on those new taxes." Her smirk faded. "Mother isn't here to keep a check on your drinking and pipe-smoking. I worry that you will fall coming home from the pub one night."

"Oh, you needn't worry, girl," Watty exclaimed. "My friend Tom Baxter always sees me home and I have found, as I age, that I am actually drinking less—nature's way of saying it's time to slow down." He shared Betsy's grin. "Besides, since last year, the National Insurance Act has enabled us to get free care from doctors."

"Life has certainly changed for the better here in England," Betsy mused.

"Well, not everyone is pleased with the changes," Watty noted. "The level of benefits are far too low for many of us poorer folk. Pensions should be universal, and not based on income. And then there are the rich folks, complaining bitterly about paying higher taxes to support people who can work but choose not to." He was speaking of the new super tax of 6d to the pound that had been introduced for those earning £5,000 or more a year. "Those dammed Conservatives might ruin all this though."

The Conservatives held a large majority in the House of Lords, and they objected to this attempt to redistribute wealth. Betsy had heard they'd planned to block the reforms. Lloyd George had toured the country making speeches to working class citizens to promote the budget. He called his budget a "war budget"—not to raise money for arms, but to wage war against poverty and squalor. In one of his speeches, George had remarked, "Before this genera-tion has passed away, we shall have advanced a great step towards that good time when poverty, and the wretchedness and human degradation which always follows in its camp, will be as remote to the people of this country as the wolves which once infected its forests."[1] He had portrayed the nobility as elite, pow-erful people wanting to protect their wealth and stop the poor from receiving their Old Age Pensions and other welfare benefits.

Watty bade her a good night when they arrived home, and Betsy climbed the stairs to her bedroom, but she was too keyed up to sleep. Excitement warred with more than a little trepidation to hold sleep at bay for a long time. Dreams of a new life swirled in her head and fed her body with an electric energy that traversed its length, tingling in her fingers and toes. She had made up her mind. Next week she would travel over to Burton and arrange for her passage to Canada. Her savings should be just enough to purchase her third class ticket, with enough left over for some material with which to sew a couple of new frocks. The last time she glanced at her clock it read 2:45. Eventually, the whirring of ideas in her brain slowed and she drifted off into a restless slumber.

* * *

Four days later, Betsy and her father stepped off the carriage and onto the road outside the Burton branch office of the White Star Line. The building that housed it was old, and a distinct musty smell struck Betsy's nostrils as they entered and closed the creaking door behind them. Betsy hesitated on the landing. "I'm not sure I can do this," she said. Watty grabbed her arm and gently shoved her toward the counter, where a grey-haired gentleman sat. He glanced up at the two as they entered, then again dropped his gaze to a newspaper open on the countertop before him.

Betsy and Watty stood, silently waiting, for several seconds. Finally Watty coughed.

The clerk looked up from the paper. "Yes?"

"Is this the right place to purchase tickets for passage to America?" asked Watty.

The man slowly folded his paper and rose. "Yes. Where do you want to go? And when were you thinking of sailing?"

Watty nudged Betsy. She felt her cheeks flush. Here she was, thinking of heading off to Canada alone, and she couldn't even begin the process of applying for immigration and booking passage on a ship! She glanced at Watty, who frowned and nodded toward the counter. He just wanted what was best for his daughter, she knew. And who knew, if this worked out for her, maybe he could join her in a year or so after all. But first she had to speak up!

"It's for me," declared Betsy in a loud, clear voice. "I want to apply for immigration to Canada and I'd like to book passage on the maiden voyage of the new ocean liner, the *Titanic*. I would also like to inquire about employment opportunities there."

The clerk slowly pulled out the necessary application papers and arranged them on the counter. "Luck must be on your side," he muttered, scanning a logbook he opened at one end of the counter. "There is still passage available on that liner's first sailing." He looked up at her. "You'll be travelling in luxury."

"I want to go in steerage, the third class section of the ship," Betsy clarified.

"Yes, of course...even third class is luxurious, compared to any of the existing liners," he assured her with a thin smile.

"So I have heard." Betsy replied.

"One minute," Watty interrupted, stepping up to the counter. "No daughter of mine is going to America in steerage," he said, his tone firm, his white brows drawn down in determination. "I will add the extra for a second class ticket."

Betsy turned to him in surprise. "Father, thank you! Second class—I can't imagine!" Then a fleeting moment of grief clouded her glee—she may never see her family and friends in England again. *Perhaps this is a mistake,* she thought, but then she saw the pride on her father's face and dismissed her fears. *This is right,* she thought, remembering the calm that had settled over her at the slide show. *I'm doing the right thing.* Her smile returned, and she gave her father's hand a quick squeeze before turning back to the clerk.

Watty watched his daughter in her animated discussion with the clerk, happy for her, but aching inside. Oh, how he would miss her!

CHAPTER FOUR:
TIME THE AVENGER

April 8, 1912

As Betsy and her friend Lucy walked into the town centre, she glanced up at the Market Hall clock to check the time—6:30 p.m.—then read the inscription: *Time, the avenger*. Betsy smiled to herself. Time did seem to have a way of determining one's destiny in so many ways. Only weeks before, she had been gainfully employed in Birmingham. Now the writing was on the wall—her time was running out. With no prospects of a husband in sight, it was time for her to move on to a life elsewhere.

They were early. Swadlincote's evening market opened at 7:00 p.m. and ran to 10:30, drawing merchants and customers from all around the region. Betsy loved to wander through the many stalls, with their seemingly endless varieties of fresh produce and useful products. She particularly enjoyed browsing the handcarts filled with bolts of cloth and notions for sewing.

"We're early yet," she said to Lucy, who hesitated, eyes on the pub they were passing.

"Shall we pass the time in the Barley Mow?" Lucy said with a smirk, nodding toward the battered wooden door.

Betsy whirled on her, mouth open in mock horror, and then giggled. "Now Lucy, you know it's not proper for young ladies of virtue to enter such places unaccompanied."

Lucy sighed. "Yes, I suppose so. How about we head over to Coppiceside, and get some sweets from the grocer's?"

Betsy nodded. "Yes, let's; there is no virtue to be lost in candy, surely."

They left Walter J. Williams Grocers sucking on sweets and returned to the market area, pausing to watch street performers—a clown and a juggler— entertaining a small crowd off to one side. "They have to be very careful about what they perform," Lucy whispered to Betsy as they watched. "Just last week the *Burton Observer* reported on a trial for a showman named John William Snape; he put on a stage play of Little Bo Peep in a booth on Derby Street and was fined for not staging the event in a patent theatre.

Betsy shook her head. "I'm glad that my pursuits are neither so risky nor so costly."

Lucy cocked her head. "What are you thinking, Betsy?"

Smiling, Betsy pulled a recent letter from her friend Ruth Collins from her pocket and read from it to Lucy: "*No one here in my new township has your talent for sewing and tatting. If you come here to Canada, I am sure you would make a comfortable living doing just that.*"

Betsy loved to sew. She made all of her own clothing and, while employed at the Turnball's, she'd made all of young Margery's frocks. Her greatest talent, however, was her tatting. Many of Birmingham's elite gentlewomen sported the lovely collars and cuffs that she created and sold for a modest price.

"That sounds like a great plan," Lucy said. "You are so talented, Betsy. I just love my collars and cuffs that you've made for me. You should be successful in Canada."

"I'm concerned that I may not be able to get needed materials," Betsy said. "Or what if the women there have different fashion tastes? I wasn't sure if that would be enough of a guarantee of employment to pass the immigration requirements."

Lucy nodded. "I see your dilemma. So how have you dealt with that?"

"Well, when I booked my passage in Burton, I signed up on the employment registry. I left open the classification, but I was told that work as a housemaid or farm assistant was guaranteed. They just got back to me yesterday and told me I would be employed as a domestic by the Brown family of Craven, Saskatchewan. I really hope they have small children, because I miss my young Margery fiercely. Now all I need is the final confirmation of my immigration status."

Lucy smiled reassuringly, then said, "Oh, look." She pulled Betsy's arm and pointed at a bolt of beautiful grey flannel displayed in one of the stalls. "This fabric would look perfect on you, Betsy."

Betsy had to agree; the material was lovely and she would feel attractive while wearing it. She inspected the material, frowning critically when she saw the merchant watching her, then bartered with the merchant for a few minutes until she was comfortable enough with the price to buy several yards of the fabric. "This will make the perfect travelling outfit," she declared to Lucy as they walked away from the stall. "I can't wait to get started on it."

They left the market at 9:00 p.m., finished with their shopping, and headed up to Alma Road. When they arrived at Betsy's home, she was surprised to find a telegram awaiting her, the yellow envelope tucked in the crack between the outside jamb and the door. It was from Nixon's Shipping Office in Burton.

"Open it, open it!" implored Lucy as they stepped inside.

Betsy opened the envelope and read aloud the message contained therein: *"Dear Miss Oakes: We regret to inform you that due to a delay in approving your application for immigration to Canada, we must change your date of departure from Southampton. The Canadian authorities have informed us that the delay should be no more than three weeks. We have rebooked you on Titanic's sister ship, the Olympic, on the next available sailing of that ship on April 22, 1912. Please accept our apology. You will still be sailing out of Southampton and the ship will depart at 12:30 a.m. Arrive at least three hours in advance to allow for sufficient boarding time."*

Betsy could not believe her eyes. It took a few minutes for the reality to sink in and when it did, she felt her face flush as her anger rose. How dare they penalize her for their delays? She had booked specifically on the *Titanic,* second class, even! And now— Overcome by a desire to lash out, she reached blindly for the nearest object and flung it against the fireplace. As it smashed into hundreds of tiny fragments, she realized, to her horror that she'd picked up the last remaining piece of her mother's rare Chinese porcelain.

The sound of shattering china brought Walter rushing down the stairs. "Whatever has gotten into you, girl?" he asked, looking from the fireplace to Betsy, his eyes wide with alarm.

"Oh Father," she wailed, "You won't believe what was in this telegram left at the door. The White Star Line had a delay in getting my immigration papers through and they went and rebooked me on their other ship, the *Olympic*. I don't believe it. I am furious! I had my hopes set on making that maiden voyage on the newest one."

Watty relaxed and walked over to put his arm around Betsy's shoulders. "Dear, dear daughter. Don't take this so hard. You know very well that when one door closes, another one opens up. It wasn't meant to be. I know you're disappointed, but life will go on. You will get to Canada. You have coped with worse things than this in your lifetime and remember, what's for you won't go by you!"

Betsy remained staring at the floor, refusing to let go of her disappointment. "Remember," he said, "the *Titanic* and the *Olympic* are nearly identical and what's more, the *Olympic* has been tried and tested and proven safe. Not that safety was an issue with either of these great ships. Both were advertised as the most "unsinkable" ships ever to set sail".

It took several hours before Betsy could calm down. "Well," she finally declared to her father, "one good thing is that the delay will give me a chance to finish sewing the dresses I need to make. I was worried I wouldn't have enough time to finish them." She offered a wan smile when Watty grinned and squeezed her shoulders, but her heart was filled with disappointment, just the same.

For the next three weeks, Betsy focused her attention on making her new dresses and on packing and then repacking her trunk and carry-on suitcase. The days passed quickly despite the delay, and with her sailing date drawing closer and closer, she could hardly contain her excitement. She was about to embark on a daring new adventure!

April 15, 1912

Betsy awoke to a banging on the front door. *Who could that be, so early?* She sleepily donned her robe and made her way down the stairs. She opened the door to find Lucy on the step, newspaper in hand, her eyes wide. "Come in, come in," Betsy urged. "Whatever are you doing over here at this ungodly hour?"

"You won't believe what has happened," Lucy said, pale and breathlessly, as she stepped inside. "The *Titanic* has apparently struck an iceberg and the ship sank last night. We just heard the news this morning and I wanted to tell you right away." Lucy held up the Burton Observer that she clutched, and Betsy read the headline: *Titanic Sunk. Many Lives Lost.*

For a moment Betsy couldn't breathe. She swayed as the implications slammed into her. "Good God," she finally gasped, "I was supposed to be on that ship!" Her knees gave way and were it not for her friend's arms reaching out to catch her, she would have collapsed on the floor.

Lucy wrapped her arms around Betsy and rocked her for what seemed like an eternity. Betsy couldn't stop shaking. She'd almost been on that ship. She'd almost been on *Titanic.*

Lucy guided her into the kitchen, where Betsy dropped into a chair at the table and covered her face with her hands.

"What's this, then?" Watty asked, arriving in the kitchen to see who'd been at the door. When Lucy showed him the newspaper headline, his eyes widened in shock and he took the newspaper to read the details. When he finished he wordlessly set the paper down on the table and squeezed Betsy's shoulder before turning away to make a pot of tea.

All three sat at the table, hands cradling their teacups, anxiously discussing the few details the newspaper had printed.

"I wonder if there were any passengers from this region," Lucy mused. "Betsy, do you know? Did they say anything when you purchased your ticket?"

"No, but it's possible," Betsy said. "There were a lot of people at the slide show at the library."

"It doesn't say here how many were rescued, or where they were taken," Watty said, eyes scanning the columns of print.

"Or what caused the accident," Betsy added, wondering if it was something that could also afflict Titanic's sister, Olympic. *That's it. I'm cancelling my trip,* she said to herself.

Each question seemed to generate a million more. They decided to head into town to find out more details of the tragedy. The trio were not alone in the fifteen-minute walk into town; most of the townsfolk congregated on High Street, or gathered on street corners, in pubs, in schoolyards, and outside of grocery shops, sharing the latest tidbit of news. Rumours abounded. Some people claimed to have relatives that either worked on building the ships or who were employed as crewmembers. Nobody claimed to have relatives on board as passengers.

No one was more affected by the whole tragic affair than Betsy. She was filled with horror and sorrow along with everyone else, but she was also overwhelmed by a huge sense of relief and gratitude, a feeling that soon generated a huge sense of guilt. She wondered why she had been spared. She wondered if she would have been rescued, had she gone on that ship. She wondered again how safe the sister ship was, given this tragedy, on board a boat that was advertised to be "unsinkable." She was due to travel in only seven short days. She wondered if she should cancel her passage.

By Thursday, April 18, more news was available concerning the sinking. The headlines of the *Burton Observer* read: ***The Titanic Founders, Loss of Life About 1,500, Rescuing Liners Pick Up 868 Souls.***[2]

Betsy still had difficulty believing what had happened. Without pausing for her usual morning coffee, she instead sat at the kitchen table, poring over the full front page of stories. One story concerned a lady from Burton who was believed to be on board the ship. She read:

Burton Lady on the Titanic. A First Class Stewardess

"As far as can be ascertained there were no local passengers on board the Titanic, *but one of the first-class stewardesses, Mrs. J. Gould, formerly lived in Burton for a number of years. Mrs. Gould is a sister of Mrs. J. Windmill of Calais Rd. and of Mr. H. Cook of Walton, and over 20 years ago lived with them by the canal side at Shobnall. Upon getting married, however, she lived in Liverpool and entered the service of the White Star Line on the death of her husband over ten years ago. She worked her way up on the vessels upon which she served, being transferred to the newer ships as they were launched. She has had some remarkable experiences, being on the* Suevic *at the time that that vessel was cut in two, whilst last year she was on the* Olympic *when the collision with the* Hawke *occurred".*[3]

Another short article concerned the ship's captain, Edward J. Smith. The plan was for Smith to retire following this sailing, having been given a healthy bonus that almost doubled his salary that year. The *Burton Observer* reported:

Captain Smith's Fate. He Intended to Retire

"Although I have no official information on the point," writes a representative, *"I am in a position to state that this was to have been Captain Smith's last voyage. As his name has not so far appeared on the list of survivors, it is feared that he is among the drowned; in fact, those that knew him best in Liverpool are confident that he went down with his ship." "Although he had passed his 60th year,"* remarked one shipping expert who knew him, *"he was as fine a specimen of the Atlantic commander as our merchant service could show."*[3]

It seems that all told, there were 350 first class, 305 second class, 800 third class passengers, and 903 crew and stewards on board the ship; the ship was carrying 3,418 sacks of mail, as well.[4]

The incident shocked the world. Every possible contributor was being blamed, and there was talk of hefty lawsuits and payouts. People were sure the White Star Line would not survive the financial fallout. That would gravely affect the whole of the British economy, as shipbuilding and related operations were a sizable component of the country's fiscal health. In the groups that still gathered on

Swadlincote's street corners and shops to discuss the latest news, emotions ranged from disbelief, to horror, to anger.

Each day brought Betsy closer to the day she would depart for Southampton. Though she had mixed feelings, she had decided to adhere to her plan to immigrate to Canada. The clock was ticking. *Is there some as-yet unknown reason why I was spared from this horrible tragedy? Is this how time was already my avenger?* she wondered. She would be sailing out on the next voyage on the *Titanic*'s sister the Olympic. Or would she? Maybe she wasn't meant to go at all.

But White Star delayed the next Olympic sailing several weeks for the company to make some modifications to the ship. Betsy was relieved and used the time to finish her sewing and make sure her father was going to be comfortable.

CHAPTER FIVE: DAY ONE ABOARD THE OLYMPIC

May 17, 1912

Betsy left the ship's deck and began excitedly searching for her room. *My life has already changed so much, I can't even find where I'm to spend the next five days of it,* she thought wryly, finally asking directions of a passing steward.

When she at last entered her cabin, she looked around at the small space and smiled. A mahogany bunk bed with fresh white linens nestled against the far wall. Next to it stood a dark mahogany bureau; when she opened its top, she found it became a writing desk, equipped with paper and pens and a small stack of postcards ready to be addressed and mailed. Two oil-burning lamps sat on top of the bureau on either side of a rectangular mirror. A tapestry-covered sofa sat against the opposite wall, with room underneath to tuck her suitcase. There was a small closet in one corner and coat hooks on the wall by the door, and a porthole to look out at the ocean. The room felt cozy yet elegant.

She had heard that the *Titanic* and *Olympic* had set entirely new standards for transatlantic travel. In fact, second class passengers were treated exactly the way first class passengers were treated on all of the other passenger liners. Her worries over the ship's safety faded somewhat at the prospect of some true pampering! Maybe she might even quell her anxiety enough to actually enjoy this trip.

She removed her coat and hung it on one of the hooks, set her carry-on case on the sofa, then tried out the bed—just the right firmness, and the sheets were deliciously smooth, almost like satin—then she peered into the bureau mirror to rearrange her hair. Satisfied that she'd familiarized herself well enough with her quarters for now, she decided to set out to explore some of the ship. Deciding now would be a good time to take a look at the first class areas, before all of the passengers were settled in, she headed immediately for the large, circular Grand Staircase; the photo she'd seen of it at the slide show had captured her fancy.

It was more spectacular in person. She stopped at its foot and let her eyes follow the steps up to the entrance to the first class reception room and dining saloon. Then she stepped onto the first step and ran her hand along the dark, rich wood of the handrail.

She looked around. Everyone appeared pre-occupied with the ship's boarding. As no one stopped her from ascending, she quickly ran up the steps.

She peeked through the doors into the reception room, where first class passengers would gather before and after dinner. Wicker chairs in groups of two and four, their comfort bolstered with decorative cushions, were clustered around small round wicker tables. Palm ferns rose six feet in the air from large clay pots. White walls and the white ceiling helped brighten the room and the ceiling was decorated with an intricate, three-dimensional plaster relief of circles, squares, diamonds, and four-leaf swirls and the walls were punctuated with stained leaded glass windows that let in outside light. The carpet was dark red with a detailed pattern of squares that made it look almost like elegant Italian ceramic tiles.

The doors to the dining room were open so she stepped inside. The room was very open, measuring, she guessed, at least 90 feet wide and about 115 feet long. Its walls were also white, decorated with detailed relief carvings. Tables were arranged for groups of two, four, six, and eight and the seats and backs of the oak chairs were upholstered in green velvet. Bay windows stretched across the outside wall, with stained glass inserts. The tables were set with an elegant china service of white and blue porcelain with detailed gold trim. She strolled closer to one table, imagining herself dining here, and noticed that the cutlery was all stamped with the White Star Line emblem.

She turned to leave and noticed a dinner menu posted by the door. *So what does the upper crust eat?* she wondered idly, stopping to read over a more elegant and complex assortment of dinner offerings than she could have ever imagined.

Suddenly feeling tired from travel and the excitement of the past weeks, Betsy decided to return to her room and lie down for a rest so she'd be fresh for dinner. She had plenty of time to explore all the other amenities on the ship in the coming days. Upon reaching her room, she closed the door and slipped off her dress. She loosened the laces of her corset and a wave of relief came over her as she realized she had gained a couple of pounds cooking for her father. As the ship pulled further away from the shore, with the orchestra playing and the faint goodbyes, and cheers, from those on shore, she heard the sound of the horn blast three times and soon, with the gentle rocking of the vessel, she drifted off.

Some time passed and suddenly Betsy awoke with a start. She looked around, disoriented for a moment, and then glanced at her watch. *Heavens! I slept for hours! The ship has been sailing for four of them!* It would soon be time for dinner; she had to change and freshen up.

She rose quickly then paused, reaching out to grip the edge of the bureau for balance. She felt nauseous, and her head throbbed with a headache. *Am I coming down with something?* She felt her forehead, which wasn't warm, but cool and damp. Then it hit her: *Seasick! I must already be suffering seasickness!* She certainly wasn't hungry. She felt so uncomfortable that the last thing she wanted to do was eat. Hoping her ill feelings would go away once she became acclimatized to the ship's gentle rocking motion, she decided to climb back into bed and wait it out.

It didn't get better, though. In fact, later that evening her leg muscles began to spasm and she seemed to be constantly swallowing saliva. On edge, frightened, she jumped when, around 8:00 p.m., she heard a knocking at the door.

"Come in," she managed. She didn't care who it was; the company of anyone would alleviate her fear, and with luck they would know how to help her. She almost wept when the door opened and Rosa her stewardess stepped inside.

One look at the young passenger and the young woman knew that Betsy was succumbing to the dreaded symptoms of motion sickness. "Have you eaten?" she asked.

"Heavens, no," Betsy groaned.

"I'll get you a tray of tea, toast, and juice," Rosa said briskly, and left. She soon returned with a lovely tray that also included a nice bowl of fresh fruit.

Betsy nibbled at a few of the items on the tray and exclaimed, "I don't know what is wrong with this food! Nothing tastes right. Not even the tea."

Rosa smiled. "When a person is seasick, the senses of smell and taste are off love. I have been on quite a few ships and find that even people who normally are reliable judges of the qualities of foods and drinks sometimes make absurd complaints and criticisms in relation to the food and drink on the ship. It's not uncommon for many passengers to leave a ship feeling quite sure that inferior wines were provided by the staff under cover of respectable labels. We have even been accused of employing incompetent cooks. Coffee and tea are common subjects of criticism."

"That's fascinating," Betsy said, and meant it, but she was not in the mood for a medical lecture. "I appreciate all these details, but I think I really need a basin beside me. I feel quite nauseous."

"Of course." Rosa left again and returned with an enamel basin. Much to Betsy's chagrin, she found it extremely useful a short time later. Rosa had also brought a damp washcloth and a fresh towel.

"Oh, thank you," Betsy said when Rosa offered them. Vomiting had left her feeling soiled and sweaty, and the cool washcloth felt wonderful.

When she was more comfortable, Rosa pulled up a chair and the two began to get to know one another.

As dusk fell that first evening, they sat engrossed in conversation.

"Where were you from originally?" queried Betsy. "I detect a bit of an Italian accent, but you were not always from there, were you?"

Rosa lifted an eyebrow. "You have a good ear. I was actually born in Austria. My father and mother were Italian, though; he emigrated from Italy in 1885 and my mother joined him the next year. They were married, and the following year I was born." Rosa smiled in memory. "We didn't have much by way of material goods in those days, but my parents were very much in love. I have memories of it being a very happy home."

"What did your father do?" Betsy asked, thinking of her own home life. Her father had spent all his life in the mines, and no one in her family had travelled far from Swadlincote until she left to work in Birmingham.

"He was a musician," Rosa answered. "Father spent his days playing his accordion in various bands and orchestras and mother and I did household chores and prepared the evening meal. I cherished my father's homecoming; I can still smell the musty door of tobacco and sweat that he bore with him every night."

Betsy smiled and nodded, thinking of the odours Watty's life had stamped on him. Funny, when she was last home, she had no longer minded the smell of stale beer and pipe tobacco, but cherished them as part of a loved one she may never see again.

"We moved around Austria as my father relocated to find work," Rosa continued. "I was sick a lot—and I didn't appreciate the three new brothers that my parents produced, one after the other!" She looked at Betsy. "Do you have brothers?"

Betsy shook her head. "There was just my sister who died a few years back, and I," Betsy said, "And I was the younger."

"We eventually moved to back to Italy and settled in a mountainous area in the north. But," Rosa added before Betsy could comment, "after my father died quite unexpectedly, we moved to France. My mother had a sister there."

"So even as a child, you were well-travelled," Betsy exclaimed. "I hadn't thought much about travelling, certainly not abroad, until my friend Ruth started sending me postcards from Canada. Then I saw glimpses of a Canada show, advertising for immigrants, and I just couldn't believe how amazing it looked. It made me feel I wasn't running away from something. I was going to a new place."

Rosa nodded. "Interesting. I guess I came by my nomadic tendencies early." Her face clouded. "Eventually my mother became employed in a pharmacy. I actually raised my youngest brother during those years, as he was quite a bit younger than I. It was hard, having Mother away at work so much of the time, and I missed my father terribly. We were very close."

Betsy nodded, thinking of her dearly departed mother and sister. "Your travels must have left you with a knowledge of several languages," she said. "Did that help you in becoming a ship stewardess?"

"It did eventually," Rosa said, "but my first post was employment as a governess for a wealthy family in France, near the town where we were living at the time."

Betsy sat up. "Why, isn't that a coincidence? We both have been employed as governesses." It was a small lie as although she engaged in a great deal of childcare, she had no training as a governess and never progressed from receiving maid's wages. But from that day forward, for the rest of her life, whenever asked about her employment in England, Betsy referred to her work there as that of a governess. The words "servant" or "maid" never made their way back into her vocabulary.

The women discovered something else they had in common in their employment: they had both been charged with identifying proper English customs, table manners, and social nuances for their respective families, both of which had come into the middle class recently and longed to be accepted by their peers.

They laughed as they recalled similar experiences when questioning the nannies and servants in neighbouring parks. Betsy confessed, "I some-times wondered if I had been fed false information as a practical joke. Some of the things they told me seemed so silly! But I had the opportunity to confirm some in a visit to the library. Did you know that most customs are holdovers from the Elizabethan era?"

"It makes sense," Rosa said. "What contemporary gentleman would *want* to wear evening dress just to eat dinner, even if there is no one present but the family?" They laughed. "I found it fascinating that the dress code for a proper English dinner is so very strict. An English lady is always to appear in semi-grand toilette," she parroted, as if reciting from a book of etiquette, "often low-necked, fully corseted, and with a corsage and elbow sleeves. And for formal dinners—oh my, for formal affairs the women must wear gloves. At least they are made so that they can be peeled back." Giggling, Rosa leapt up and flounced around the room as if showing off her fine English dinner attire.

Betsy laughed, then added her own bit of humour: "Oh, and the significance placed on the lowly salt and pepper! The importance of a guest is determined by how far he or she is seated from the salt and pepper. And it's the only thing the diners pass themselves, *always* together, even if only the salt was asked for."

"And *always* to the right, even if the person on your left requested them," a chuckling Rosa chimed in. "Heaven help the person on your left!"

"Which is probably why the guest of honour is always to be seated on the host's right," Betsy said.

"Yet his wife must be on the hostess's *left*," Rosa mused. "Something of a snub to the wife, to have to wait so long for the salt and pepper."

Both women burst into gales of laughter. When Betsy, who was now forgetting about her nausea recovered, she said, "I wonder what the reasoning was behind the rule that no wife is to be seated next to her husband?"

Rosa snorted. "Have you seen some married couples together? It was likely preferred!" More gales of laughter.

"The children are the fortunate ones," Betsy said. "Given the choice between such fussy rules and taking my meals in the nursery with their nanny or governess, most would choose the nursery!"

"Well, you might eat more quickly that way, "Rosa interjected. "The children don't have to wait until the host begins or signals the guests to start eating. What if your host were more a talker than an eater? You might starve, waiting for him to shut up!"

"And even then, you have to mind that you're holding the utensils correctly—as important as using the right utensil for each course," Betsy said.

"And when asked if you prefer clear or thick soup, you must reply promptly and once served, eat noise-lessly, with the spoon in the right hand, scooping the soup away from you," Rosa added primly, once more proving her mastery of the rules of etiquette.

"Pity the poor people that are left-handed," remarked a giggling Betsy. But then she sobered. *Would the same rules hold true in the Olympic's second class dining room?* she wondered. When she asked Rosa, she was relieved when the stewardess shook her head.

"Second class is much more down to earth," she assured Betsy. "As long as one doesn't belly up to the table as if about to eat from a trough, no eyebrows should lift."

Betsy laughed as much in relief as in appreciation of Rosa's quip.

"I often wondered why the servants always made the rounds of the table in pairs—as much to restrain an over-eager diner as to offer the various dishes, condiments and wines."

Again Rosa snorted, containing a guffaw. "Oh, heavens no, that's because no guest can ever pass a plate or help themselves to anything," Rosa sing-songed. "That might suggest base origins."

"Yet the master is allowed to sometimes carve a roast or bird," Betsy mused. "You would think that would suggest origins more base than taking a helping from a server."

"And bread has to be passed by the servants and always broken, never cut..." Betsy shook her head. "The rules one must remember - simply to eat! And the signals learned—the servant must understand that you're *refusing* wine by saying simply 'Thanks,' not requesting some."

"Ah, the denial," Rosa drawled, grinning. "The hostess always has to pretend everything is perfect, even when it's burned or the cook used too much salt."

"Yes!" Betsy giggled.

"One time our cook cooked a pork roast so long it was dry and tasteless and it was hilarious, watching everyone pretending to eat it, but spending more time playing with their utensils!"

"Oh, the utensils," Betsy said. "My employer was quite concerned that their silverware and linens were top-notch, which was the norm, even in less affluent families. And God forbid if a guest should fold their napkin up at the end of the meal and place it on their plate. That would imply that the hostess would reuse the napkin without laundering it."

Both women sniggered, then Betsy finished in a haughty tone, "One is to leave it loose at the side of the plate." Then she frowned. "I never did understand why plum pudding or a fresh tart might be served in the middle of dinner, before the game."

"Well, at least in North American households, the salad is served first, instead of last with the cheese."

Betsy cocked her head. "Is it?"

They traded a few more upper class absurdities, laughing, and then both of them fell silent. Such silences often preface a transition to a more intimate level of interaction, and sure enough, after a moment, Rosa quietly turned to Betsy and asked, "I know this will change the topic, but I have a rather personal question. Did you ever have the master of the house behave inappropriately with you?"

Betsy could not look her in the eye. She most certainly *had* had such experiences! Looking back, she was deeply ashamed at how she had handled Charles' initial advances, though she'd grown to care for him deeply as time passed. She had no training on how to deal with such things, leaving her, as an employee, feeling vulnerable and powerless at first. *Strange,* she thought, *I was able to rebuke the advances of that horrid friend of my father's, back at age nineteen. But more recent events concerning my employer...that turned out quite differently. Perhaps time, the time for actually coming to know and admire the man, had been the key. And love,* she thought. Her heart still ached at the thought of his warm embraces.

She was not sure how much she should divulge, and decided to test Rosa out first. "Yes, I did. I was not sure how to handle the situation. How about you? What have you experienced?" Turning the question back onto the questioner was a clever way of avoiding an immediate answer, she had discovered.

Rosa flushed a little. "No, but my roommate told me about an experience she had. She said her employer never seemed comfortable unless he had a gun in his hand and was out looking for foxes or other game. One night when the wife was out, the master sidled up to my friend and complimented her on her dress. Then he ran his hands over her waist and began groping her buttocks."

"Oh my," Betsy interjected. "He was forward, wasn't he?"

Rosa nodded. "It's not that uncommon, for young girls in service to be treated this way. What was your experience?"

Betsy hesitated. She knew she liked this young stewardess. In fact, she even reminded Betsy a little of her sister. In their younger days they had been close...until at age 15 Betsy's sister was convinced to marry a neighbour's boy. But the guilt of Betsy's former relationship with her employer lay heavily in her heart. And no matter how much they had laughed together about silly upper class etiquette, this was a very personal thing to share with a woman she'd just met. And yet...she felt this unexplained closeness to Rosa, who also seemed to feel likewise.

Betsy focused on an imaginary speck of lint on her knee as she spoke. "Well, I had been in service with my employers, the Turnballs, for about six months. The Missus was quite ill following the birth of her daughter, and she remained in hospital for several weeks. When she came home, she was different. She was withdrawn, angry, and often stayed in her room for days on end. I began sitting up nights talking to the master in front of the fireplace. One evening after the baby was tucked in bed and I was washing up and changing into my nightclothes, I turned to find the master standing in my room. He was crying. I put on a robe and asked him to sit down on a chair while I perched on the edge of the bed."

Betsy looked up. Rosa's eyes were wide, but she didn't interrupt, only nodded once in encouragement.

"He was very distraught," Betsy continued, abandoning the imaginary lint. "He told me how he and his wife were becoming estranged and how he was having many impure thoughts about me. I really had come to admire this man and, as wrong as I knew it was, I wanted to comfort him and ease his pain in some way." She shifted, crossing her ankles. "He came to me on occasion after that, over the ten years of my service there. In the end, I had to leave. I had come to love him and the little girl, but they were not mine to love." She looked directly at Rosa. "I am not proud of this and will likely never tell another soul. I guess it filled a need in both of us. I wish now I had some of your firm resolve. I admire your strength so much, Rosa."

Rosa winced just a little and Betsy wondered about the sadness crossing her face so fleetingly, a sign that there was surely more to Rosa's life than what she had shared with Betsy. Before either could say more, Betsy surprised herself with a huge yawn.

She realized the feeling of sickness in her gut was coming back. Her face turned pale.

"You are tired and feeling ill," Rosa said, rising. "I will leave you to get some rest and come by in the morning. Be prepared for another day or two of sea sickness," she warned, and Betsy realized their conversation had taken her mind completely off of her discomfort. "The seas are predicted to be quite rough tonight. I will try and take you for a walk outside tomorrow. That sometimes helps."

"Thank you, Rosa," Betsy said, and meant it. "Good night." Again she noticed the sadness in the stewardess's eyes as she said good night, and made a mental note to ask her about it the next time they talked, if possible. There was so much about each other that they still did not know.

* * *

Rosa closed the door to Betsy's stateroom and leaned her back against the wall beside it for a few moments, glad the corridor was empty. *I wonder if the young Englishwoman would respect me half as much, if she knew my whole story,* she thought to herself.

CHAPTER SIX:
ROSA'S GRUESOME
DISCOVERY

The next morning, as Rosa had predicted, Betsy was again feeling absolutely miserable. The ship had encountered a violent storm around two a.m., waking her to spend the rest of the night with dry heaves and shivering.

After bringing her sympathy and a breakfast tray, which again Betsy barely touched, Rosa moved on to tend to her other charges on Deck 5. The first was Mrs. Bernice Vaughn and her nine-year-old daughter, Louisa, in the cabin next to Betsy's.

"Good morning," said Rosa when the curious youngster answered the door. "I've come to make up your room and see if you have any unmet needs."

"Oh, do come in," the young girl said, stepping back and opening the door wider.

Rosa looked about the room and sighed. It was a total disaster. Clothes were scattered everywhere, shoes were strewn across the floor, and bottles of perfume and assorted jewellery lay on the unmade bed. She dreaded cleaning such rooms, as inevitably something would seem to go missing; on one occasion, at least, she had been accused of theft. "Would you like to tidy up your things before I make up your room?" she asked the mother.

"No, just come in and get started," replied Mrs. Vaughn. "We'll leave and go for our breakfast."

They departed and Rosa began the onerous task of sorting out the myriad items, folding clothing or hanging garments on the hooks provided on the wall. She gathered the items on the bed and arranged them neatly on top of the bureau.

That was when she spotted the opened diary. It wasn't like she was snooping—she didn't even have to open it. It was lying open, and the last entry caught her eye:

> *May 18, 1912. We are out at sea now. The farther we are from the horrid scene by the canal, the better I am feeling. I know I was angry that night, but I never intended to push him into the water like that. I am still not convinced that he did not slip. I can't get the sight of the body slipping below the surface out of my mind. I wonder if anyone has reported him missing yet. I hope I will be able to sleep soon. I don't know what would happen to*

poor Louisa if ever I lost my temper with her. I seem to almost black out and lose complete control over my actions. Maybe in the new world I can seek some help for my violent temper.

Rosa stepped back as if shoved, staring at the open book. In her four years at sea, she had never encountered a situation like this. Murder! Violence! What was she to do? Though horrified, she busied herself finishing up the cleaning; she didn't want Mrs. Vaughn to suspect that she knew and she closed the diary.

Finally Rosa stepped out into the hall, grateful that the woman and her daughter had not returned while she was still inside—how would she face the woman, with what she now knew? But what *should* she do?

I've got to talk to someone about this, she thought. *If I don't, I'll go crazy with worry. Betsy. She's just next door, and I should alert her to the possibility of danger anyway.*

Decided, she stepped over and knocked on Betsy's door.

"Come in," Betsy called, and she opened the door and stepped inside to find Betsy lying on the bed, her face pale and drawn, her eyes sunk within dark circles. "Do come in, Rosa," she said, and then frowned. "You look shaken. Is something wrong?"

Rosa wondered if she should go on. Coupled with their frank talk late into the evening before, this would be getting too close to crossing the line between employee and guest. Only this morning the head of housekeeping had warned the staff of the rules regarding fraternizing with the ship's passengers. Rosa swallowed. "May I sit down?"

"Of course you may. Pull up that chair over there. I wanted to thank you again for the breakfast tray. I wish I could have eaten more of it. It really did look good."

Rosa pulled up a chair and crossed her arms on her chest. "I'm sorry you're still not feeling well," She said, her mind working through how best to broach the real reason for her visit. There was a moment of silence. *Just say it,* Rosa told herself. *Worry about crossing lines when the subject isn't so potentially dangerous!* "Miss Oakes, I need to talk about an incident that occurred a short time ago."

"Please, call me Betsy."

Rosa smiled. "Betsy. I likely shouldn't even be speaking to you about such things, but somehow I sense you can be trusted to deal with a very sensitive matter."

Betsy sat upright in bed, leaning forward, eyes wide. "Oh yes. Please do go on."

"Well I accidently came across another passenger's diary this morning, lying open on the bureau," she added, so Betsy didn't think she'd been snooping. "In it was a very suspicious confession of what sounded like a crime...well, a murder, to be exact."

Betsy gasped. "Murder? Are you certain?"

"Well, no. I can't be certain. But there was mention of a body going into a canal and fears were expressed about what would happen if the writer lost control due to anger again. I just don't know what I should do."

"Why wouldn't you go straight to the ship's head of security?" Betsy asked.

"I've been thinking about doing that. But if I do, it would appear as though I've been snooping in a passenger's private diary. That is something that is strictly forbidden."

Betsy nodded. "Well, is there anyone who might be at risk if you don't report this?"

Rosa thought for a moment. "If I say nothing, the woman might get away with murder. Her little girl may be at risk as well, given that the woman suffers from severe fits of uncontrollable anger, by her own admission. There is a chance other passengers may be at risk too. Really, I must do something. I just wish I had more evidence that a real crime was committed."

"Hmm, maybe I can help you. I could do a little sleuthing and she would not suspect I knew anything of her crime. Which cabin is this person in?"

"Well, as a matter of fact, she's right next door to you." *Why did I say that?* Rosa knew she had crossed the line, but it was too late. Now all she could do was avoid compounding it by not involving Betsy too much. "But I couldn't ask that of you. There would be too much risk if she sensed anything. And you are feeling so ill. No, it's out of the question. I just need to devise a plan for myself, one that won't land me in hot water for being a snoop."

Rosa stood and quickly bade Betsy farewell. She stepped into the hallway to move on with her morning duties, filled with regret and still troubled.

By noon, as she stood with the other stewardesses and stewards in an alcove behind the kitchen where they took their meal breaks—they were without so much as a chair to sit on for a rest—Rosa was still in a quandary about what she should do. She was halfway through a bun filled with cheese when her room-mate, Olga, a woman of forty-five from Holland, sidled up to her. "How's your day going, Rosa?" the woman asked in her thick Dutch accent.

Rosa hesitated. "Not very well. Not well at all," she said more decisively, then lowered her voice. "I need to ask you something."

Olga shifted closer and turned her back toward the others for privacy. "Go on."

"If you discovered that a passenger may have been involved in a serious crime, say murder, would you feel obligated to report this to security on board the ship? Suppose the crime was committed before the ship sailed," she clarified.

Olga thought for a moment. "It all depends. If I thought that anyone on board the ship was in danger, I certainly would." She paused, frowning in thought, then nodded. "Yes, I guess I would report it. It would be out of my hands then, and security could do with the information as they wished. Why do you ask?"

Rosa dropped her voice further as she replied, "I came upon some incriminating evidence regarding one of the passengers. It was...in a private diary." Olga lifted an eyebrow, and Rosa quickly added, "It was lying open on her bureau, so you see why I am reluctant to divulge the information."

Olga nodded. "Yes, I see your dilemma. So what will you do?"

Rosa sighed. "I just don't know yet. I'll definitely take your advice into account. I just need to think some more. Surely I'll make a decision by the end of the day."

"Yes, best not to leave it too long," Olga said.

That afternoon, Rosa was glad to see Mrs. Vaughn's name on the list of her guests who had requested afternoon tea delivered to their room. Perhaps she could turn it into an opportunity to find out more.

Betsy, of course, was another room service recipient. Rosa took in her tray of egg salad sandwiches, scones with whipped butter, thick whipped crème and strawberry jam, and silver tea service before attending to Mrs. Vaughn.

Betsy sat up in her bed when Rosa entered. "What news in the murder mystery?" she asked as Rosa set her tray down. "Have you decided what to do?"

Rosa sighed. "Not yet. If only there were more to go on than that diary."

"I understand your problem," Betsy said. "You don't want to earn a reprimand or worse, only because you were trying to do the right thing."

Rosa nodded, grateful that Betsy understood. "Perhaps I'll learn more. If I haven't found out more by this evening, though, I believe I'll have no choice but to report it, just to be safe."

Betsy nodded. "Good luck with that, Rosa."

"Thank you. Is there anything else I can help you with?" Rosa asked.

Betsy scanned her tray. "No, this looks lovely. Thank you."

Rosa smiled and left her stateroom. *Now for Mrs. Vaughn,* she thought, smoothing the front of her skirt before knocking at the door. *Just act natural. Don't let on.* When she heard the called invitation, she lifted the tray from her cart and entered.

Mrs. Vaughn again had the bureau set up as a writing desk and was seated before it. She looked up as Rosa entered. "Why, good afternoon. Come on in. You can put the tray down on the footstool here. I just want to finish this letter home, but will have my tea in few minutes."

Rosa complied and looked around the room as she straightened. She didn't see young Louisa, Mrs. Vaughn's daughter. "Where is your daughter this afternoon?" she inquired.

Mrs. Vaughn didn't look up from her letter. "Oh, she met some other children at breakfast this morning and she has been away playing with them ever since." She turned in her chair toward Rosa. "It's given me time to get caught up on a few things, so I am glad. Before now she has been hanging around me constantly, and it was really starting to grate on my nerves."

Rosa nodded as though she quite understood, but inside she felt a jolt of fear. Had the child angered her mother somehow and thus met some disastrous fate? If so, would it come to light that she, Rosa, could have prevented this, had she only told someone of her ominous find that morning? Rosa was beside herself with worry. "How nice," she managed to say, and quickly left the cabin.

That's it, she decided as soon as she was back in the corridor. She had to report her suspicions to the chief of security.

* * *

Betsy had managed to sit up on the side of her bed and taken a few bites of the sandwich that Rosa had delivered, but she was preoccupied with Rosa's dilemma. *I have to do something. If I can also offer evidence of the woman's misdeed, then Rosa will not be accused of invading the woman's privacy. If I, a passenger, were to present the diary as proof—no, that won't work;*

how would I explain how I came by it? She decided that nothing would be accomplished here, sitting on the edge of her bed. *I must go next door and see if that woman acts at all suspicious. Maybe I can gain her confidence and maybe even get her to confess to me.*

Betsy rose carefully and paused, assessing her stability. She felt better than she had even hours ago, and her legs seemed ready to support her. *Yes, I can do this. I will be fine. I won't stay long.* In fact, if necessary, she could claim a recurrence of the seasickness and make a quick exit from the woman's stateroom.

She dressed, put up her hair, and inspected herself in the mirror. *Still pale, but perhaps she'll think that's my natural complexion.* She pinched both cheeks to bring some colour to them, then after refastening her corset and putting on her dress, slipped out into the hallway and knocked on her neighbour's door.

A woman opened the door and asked, her tone slightly annoyed, "Yes?"

"Hello," Betsy said, "I am your next door neighbour. Betsy Oakes is the name." She extended her hand.

The woman briefly shook it. "Mrs. Bernice Vaughn," she said sharply. "Is there something I can do for you? I'm in the middle of some work."

Betsy hesitated. "Well, I just wondered if you wanted a little company while you had your tea."

"I don't really have time to visit," Mrs. Vaughn began, but then changed her mind. "Well, I suppose it wouldn't hurt me to take a short break. Come in."

As Betsy stepped into the room, Mrs. Vaughn moved to gather some loose papers off the chair and invited Betsy to sit down. Surreptitiously casting her eyes about the room as she settled in the offered chair, Betsy spotted a small brown book on the desk. It looked very much like it could be a diary, and she thought again of sneaking it out with her, if an opportunity arose. But it seemed unlikely that that would happen. The cabin was small. Its occupant sat down facing her.

Betsy tried to break the ice. "How have you found the voyage so far?"

The older woman sighed. "Well, I am travelling with my young daughter, and up until today she has been quite a handful. I had hoped to get more work done. How about you? Are you having a good time?"

Betsy had not wanted the attention turned on her, but she replied, "Well, actually, I have been quite ill ever since we set sail. Only just now have I started to get my sea legs. I hope it doesn't come back to haunt me the rest of the trip. I have been looking forward to exploring the ship and meeting some of the other passengers. Why are you going to America?"

Mrs. Vaughn avoided Betsy's eyes. She'd obviously touched a nerve. Finally the older woman said, "I've left my husband. He'd been unfaithful to me in recent years and I decided to join my sister in New York and make a new life for my daughter and myself. He wasn't too pleased, I can assure you, but we came anyway." Now Mrs. Vaughn lifted her chin and looked at Betsy. "Hurt his ego, I think, that he couldn't have his cake and eat it too."

Left him, or murdered him? Betsy wondered. "That must have made him quite angry," she said.

"Yes and no. He acted hurt and cried at first, but then yes, he did carry on and have a yelling fit at one point." Mrs. Vaughn sighed. "I am just so glad to have that chapter of my life behind me." She leaned forward in interest. "Now, how about you? Why are you running off to America all on your own?"

Again, the conversation would shift, just when she felt she was getting somewhere concerning the possible crime. *I'll have to turn it back somehow.* "I completed almost ten years of service as a governess near Birmingham and I just decided, if I was ever to have a chance at marriage and a family, I had best leave England and start over. I am heading for Canada. I have a friend who has settled there and has been begging me to immigrate."

The door flew open and a young girl burst into the room, startling Betsy. "Hi Mommy," she said breathlessly. Her hair was tussled and her clothing somewhat in disarray. "I've had a wonderful day! I met some great girls and boys and we had all kinds of games and treats. I can't wait to go back tomorrow."

Belatedly noticing Betsy, she stopped and stared. "Oh, who are you?"

"I'm your next door neighbour. I've just been having a lovely chat with your mom. My name is Miss Oakes. And what might your name be?"

"I'm Louisa."

Her mother stood and went to the sink to get a wet facecloth to wipe the child's face. As both turned away, Betsy saw her chance—she reached over and grabbed the diary from the desk. She hid it in the folds of her dress and took a deep breath. "Well, I can see you two will be busy getting ready for dinner," she said, rising abruptly, holding her skirt where it concealed the diary as if smoothing the material. "So I should go back to my cabin. It has been so nice to meet you, Mrs. Vaughn. I do hope we will meet again."

Distracted, Mrs. Vaughn glanced up and smiled quickly. "Yes, I'm sure we will. Thank you for dropping by."

Returning the smile, Betsy slipped out the door and quickly re-entered her own cabin. She pulled the diary from its hiding place and decided it best to conceal it until she could share it with Rosa. She looked around her cabin. *Under the mattress.* She walked over to the bed on shaky legs, until her knees gave out and she collapsed onto the bed. Hands shaking, she pushed the book under the mattress and reached for the bottle of seasickness medicine Rosa had brought for her. Ignoring the teaspoon beside it, she uncapped the bottle and tipped a mouthful down her throat, then flopped back onto the bed, waiting for it to take effect. It didn't take long—either that, or her visit with Mrs. Vaughn had exhausted her, because within minutes, Betsy was fast asleep. The remains of her tea tray sat uneaten.

* * *

Thinking to share thoughts with Betsy, Rosa peeked in on her ailing passenger after finishing her rounds but, seeing Betsy was fast asleep, she decided to look for the ship's security officer. There was nothing else for it but to confess to what she'd seen and hope it would be for the best.

She found Officer Grenwall in his office on the bridge deck, seated with his feet propped up on the desk. He stood and motioned for her to sit down in the chair on the other side of the desk. "What can I do for you?" he inquired, his voice lightly accented. He was a dark-skinned gentleman in his early fifties, with bushy eyebrows. Rosa guessed that he, or his ancestors, were originally from India. He wore a dark green suit with the White Star insignia sewn onto the right lapel.

Rosa wasn't sure how to begin. "Well, I came across some information today that has caused me great worry, and I feel I need to pass it on to you." She paused. He nodded encouragingly. "I was cleaning a passenger's room this morning and accidently read an entry in her diary that sent a chill down my spine."

He frowned. "Accidentally?"

"The book lay open on the bureau," Rosa hastened to say. "It was open at the page containing the entry."

Officer Grenwall nodded again. "I see." He leaned his elbows on his desk and steepled his fingers. "Go on. What did it say?"

"It made reference to a man—at least I assume it was a man—being drowned in a canal. The writer seemed to think she had pushed the person into the canal in a fit of anger and wondered if the body had been found yet. I am mostly concerned because she has a small daughter and in her diary, she makes mention of the fact that she worries that she might harm the girl if her temper is unleashed."

One of Grenwall's eyebrows rose.

Rosa continued. "There is more. When I went to take her some afternoon tea, I noticed the girl was not there in the room with her. I asked about her whereabouts and she claimed not to have seen the girl since breakfast. That was seven hours ago. She showed no concern and in fact seemed relieved that the girl was not there. I am worried and thought I should report these events to you."

Grenwall leaned back. "Well, you did the right thing. Our first issue of concern is for the girl, of course. Can you give me a complete description of her appearance?" He opened a drawer in the desk and took out a pen and paper.

"Yes, of course. She's about four feet, eight inches tall. She has long reddish hair and when I last saw her this morning, it hung in two braids down her back. She has greenish eyes and a lovely wide smile. She was wearing a pale yellow frock over a lace pinafore. I noticed one of her eye teeth was missing." Rosa paused in thought. "Now that I think of it, she also had a small scar on her right cheek." She looked at Grenwall in alarm. "Oh my, I hope it wasn't from some angry outburst by her mother."

Officer Grenwall looked up from his notes. "Now, don't worry, miss. We will get onto it right away. What was the mother's name and stateroom number?"

"Her name is Mrs. Bernice Vaughn and they occupy Stateroom 514 in the second class section. Her daughter's name is Louisa."

What exactly was going through the officer's mind, Rosa could not tell. He remained expressionless. He rose, thanked her, and said he would look into it immediately.

Rosa made her way back to her section of the ship. As she passed the first class dining saloon she could smell the aromas of dinner wafting into the hallway. Fresh mutton roast, pork loin roast, sweet potatoes in honey and butter...her mouth watered. She thought of the meagre dinner that awaited her at the end of her shift. She was due for shore leave after this voyage, and could not wait to get back home to visit her mother and her aunt in France. Nothing could touch her mother's home cooking.

* * *

The information that Stewardess Molson had brought to his attention disturbed Officer Grenwall. If there was a murderer aboard, or if a child might be in danger, it was his duty to take appropriate steps. However, so far the evidence was all circumstantial. The first thing he needed to do was determine if there were a body or a missing person that might fit the bill back in England.

He began by asking the wireless operator to check with Scotland Yard to see if there had been a body found in a canal, or if a suspicious missing person report had been filed. The quick answer back was no, not at this point. In fact, Scotland Yard's message read *No suspicious missing persons, no unidentified bodies, all-quiet on the home front for a change*.

Still there was that incriminating diary entry, and the possibility that a child might be in danger. Grenwall put his feet up on the desk and leaned back in his chair to think. His job on the ship was normally limited to dealing with the occasional unruly passenger or following up on a report of some sort of petty theft. He'd never had to worry about a murder, or anything resembling one. He wasn't sure where to begin. *If only there was more proof of an actual crime being committed,* he thought. He decided to approach the issue head on and conduct an interview with the suspect at once. He rose and headed down to Deck 5.

Standing outside Stateroom 514, Grenwall could hear voices within. One sounded like a child. *Thank heaven for that,* he thought, and knocked.

An attractive woman in her mid-thirties opened the door. "Hello. May I help you?"

"I'm Officer Grenwall, the ship's security officer, Mrs. Vaughn. I have to ask you a question or two. Would this be a suitable time to have a word?"

"Certainly," she said. "We were just readying ourselves for dinner. Do come in." She stepped back.

Grenwall stepped inside and glanced around, smiling at a girl of about nine or ten who stared at him from the far side of the room. *Her daughter, no doubt.* The child seemed unharmed, and not fearful, as one might be who had been threatened or traumatized in some way. *Good.* He turned back to Mrs. Vaughn.

"Yes, well, I wanted to know if you had—well I mean, have you...um." He just wasn't sure how to go about asking her if she had in fact killed someone. For one thing, she looked less like a murderess than almost anyone he had ever met. For another, it was almost impossible to broach the subject without giving Stewardess Molson away and making her look like a busybody. He tried again. "Mrs. Vaughn,

I know how difficult it must be to be a woman these days, if someone is treating you badly. I would not blame some women if they retaliated, even committed a crime in order to get even, if they were being beaten or abused in some way." He paused. When she said nothing, he asked, "Have you had any of those types of experiences?"

Mrs. Vaughn's eyebrows rose. "Why no, not at all. I have led a pretty sheltered life, actually. Well, up until my recent separation that is. Why would you ask such a question?"

He had no choice now. He had to divulge the source of his concern. "Mrs. Vaughn, you left your diary open this morning and without meaning to pry, the stewardess noticed a comment in it about a body in a canal. She felt just awful coming to tell me about it, but her only concern was for your young daughter. She did the right thing, but I need to follow up to determine the truth of the matter."

Mrs. Vaughn surprised him by letting out a hearty laugh. "Oh sir," she gasped between guffaws, "that wasn't my diary the young woman read. It was a page in the latest novel I am writing. I am a crime fiction writer, and my publisher has been after me to submit a manuscript as soon as I arrive in New York. That's what I'm working on now!"

Officer Grenwall breathed a huge sigh of relief. "Mrs. Vaughn, I apologize profusely—"

She waved his concern away. "In any other circumstance I would be angry, but in fact it is good to know that your staff are keeping an eye out for our children—and that the passage the stewardess read was believable enough to cause concern!"

Grenwall rose to leave, and then paused at the door with a final thought. "May I have a look at the book you are writing? I just want to be able to tie up loose ends, you understand, madam."

"Of course. No problem." She turned to take the book from her desk. Frowning in perplexity, she lifted several papers, then bent down to look underneath, to see if it had fallen on the floor. She straightened and turned to Officer Grenwall, still frowning. "I'm sorry. It was here all afternoon. I've been working on the novel today—for the first time since we set sail, actually. I can't imagine where it has disappeared to."

Grenwall's eyebrow also rose. He hated unfinished business. If only she could produce the half-written novel, he wouldn't have to go on her say-so. *Is she concealing the real record of a crime?* he wondered. He too bent down, looking under the bed and all around the room. Clearly the book had disappeared.

"Was there anyone else in your room that could have taken your manuscript, Mrs. Vaughn?" he queried. He knew Stewardess Molson would not trespass that far. Besides, if she had taken it she would have shown it to him.

"No." She put her hands on her hips and lowered her head in thought. "The only one here was the lovely young lady in the next cabin. But she would have no reason to walk away with it." She sighed. "I am very sorry about this. I really wanted to clear up any doubts you might have about the situation. I'm not sure what to do."

Grenwall suddenly noticed tears welling in the woman's eyes. Seeing that her daughter looked alarmed, Grenwall felt terrible. He fumbled for the doorknob, and then turned. "Mrs. Vaughn, I really do believe that you are innocent of any crime. Truly. I will leave you for now, and when the book turns up, please just give me a shout. I did not mean to upset you." He opened the door and slipped quickly into the hallway.

He muttered to himself as he made his way down the hall and back up to his tiny office. "Thank heaven I did not have to arrest the woman here on the ship. It would have been mighty awkward. I must find the stewardess and let her know this all turned out to be a mistake. I know she will be relieved. Still, I wish I had seen that manuscript."

* * *

Rosa came by at dinner, bringing Betsy a tray stocked with light but delicious fare. As she set the tray down, Betsy yawned and slowly sat up. "Oh, thank you, Rosa. I must have been sleeping for the past hour. That medicine you gave me can sure cause drowsiness."

"Yes, that is definitely one of the main side effects. But it's effective. It helps your stomach to settle. The ship is still rocking quite a bit."

Rosa couldn't stay long but said she would try to come back at the end of the night, when her duties were over. Still drowsy, Betsy didn't think to say anything about the diary. In fact, she fell back asleep after eating from the tray, and slept right through the night.

CHAPTER SEVEN:
THE KINDNESS OF
STRANGERS

May 19, 2012

Betsy remained in her room, though she was able to get up and stand at the sink in the morning without first taking the seasickness medicine, so she knew she was starting to get over her illness. It rained all day so she was content to stay in her room and nap on and off, but by evening, she decided it was time to venture out for dinner. She washed, brushed her long auburn hair and after braiding it, wrapped the braids across to form a crown on top. She then put on a plain long black dress that she had packed for the trip. She added a set of black and white embroidered collar and cuffs. *Not too bad for an old maid,* she thought, as she looked at herself sideways in the mirror on her way to the door.

On her way to the second-class dining salon, she passed by the men's smoking room, where after dinner drinks and cigars were enjoyed, and paused to look through the glass door. It was decorated in Louis XVI style, with oak panelling and dado rails. She'd read that linoleum tiles had been specially designed for this room. It had a very masculine feel to it, somewhat akin to what she imagined the English private men's clubs would look like.

Next to the smoking room was the library, where the women would gather after meals and indeed, it was as grand as the first class library Betsy had seen upstairs. Large windows were covered in lavish silk fabric and the luxurious Wilton rug made the room feel snug and warm. She looked forward to taking her after-dinner coffee there, if she felt up to it.

As she entered the dining hall she was surprised and delighted to find that it was almost identical to the one she had seen in first class, when she'd first boarded the ship. Like the first class dining room, it spanned the width of the ship, thereby allowing natural light to come in through large porthole windows on each side. It would seat over two thousand people at one sitting, she guessed. Sidelights in the oak panelling added elegance, as did the mahogany swivel chairs with crimson upholstery that were bolted to the floor. The tables were set with white china with a pattern of dainty blue flowers around the edges and the White Star Line logo in the centre of each piece. She was delighted to see a piano in the centre of the room.

A large placard beside the entrance displayed the menu for the evening. Following a first course of consommé with tapioca, passengers were offered their choice of baked haddock, curried chicken, lamb with mint sauce, or roast turkey with cranberry sauce. A range of vegetables was also offered. For dessert: plum pudding, wine jelly, a coconut sandwich, American ice cream, assorted nuts, fresh fruit, and cheese and biscuits. Betsy was sure no one would leave this hall feeling hungry. She knew for sure she wouldn't.

She moved farther into the room, looking about for a place to sit. Three young women seated at one table invited her to join them, and Betsy gratefully sank into an empty chair. Everyone introduced themselves. The women were travelling together, Betsy learned.

"Where are you travelling to?" she asked.

"To New York, to attend college," Mavis replied eagerly. "I plan to study to become a teacher, while Elizabeth and Jane here are going to do general studies until they decide on a career."

"That must be exciting for you," replied Betsy. "As for me, I am going to Canada. I plan to work there."

"You are brave, to be heading off on your own like that," said Mavis. "I don't think I'd have left, if there weren't the three of us. Elizabeth and I have been friends since grammar school, and Janie is Elizabeth's cousin."

ELAINE GALLAGHER

"You know, I was originally scheduled to travel on the *Titanic*," Betsy said. "You can imagine my horror and relief when I heard of the sinking."

The girls gasped. Blonde-haired Elizabeth said, "You must have been terrified to come on this ship. We were sure afraid to, after hearing of the tragedy. Our parents did a lot of checking to see what precautions had been taken to avoid another disaster by this shipping company. We almost cancelled our voyage. I bet many did."

They lamented the extent of the losses, then moved on to talking about their families back home.

"What kind of work did your father do in England?" asked Mavis.

"He was a collier," Betsy replied. "He worked his whole life in the coal mines. It was a tough job."

"It is hard work," Jane agreed. "My father was a miner in Ireland. The worst times we had were when he was on strike. Strikes created great havoc in Ireland in the past few years."

"Strikes created hardship for us, as well," Betsy agreed.

"The thing I remember most about the strikes was how people rallied together when times were tough, and food and other supplies were running out," Jane said. "Even in the great potato famines, some folks survived due the kindness of strangers and friends alike."

Betsy nodded. How well she knew about the kindness of strangers in tough times! "Would you like to hear a story about the worst strike in the history of English mining?" she asked.

"Oh please tell us," pleaded Elizabeth. "We are all history buffs and love hearing about these things."

This happened nearly eighteen years ago," Betsy began. "The strike occurred right in my region of Swadlincote, in 1893. I was only eleven at the time, but I remember it vividly, as we were all deeply affected by it. It began when the mine owners decided that the coal mining cost was too high and they announced plans to cut the wages of the miners by twenty-five percent. This caused an uproar, especially in our part of the town, since the workers there had already had their hours cut and they were having trouble feeding their families. My Father would come home looking so sad on most days. That's when he started spending more and more time at the pub, in fact," she recalled.

"In late July, the men went out on strike, thinking it would be a short time until the mine owners gave in. Instead, non-union workers were recruited and that's when the violence started to erupt. The mine owners had to bring in outside police reinforcements to deal with the situation. People were getting desperate for food. Those with gardens were best off; they shared what they had, but it was only a short-term solution. We had no garden. I still remember the day when my Father came home with a dead sheep in his arms. 'Where did that come from?' asked Mama. 'It was loose on the road, down by the schoolyard. I reckon anything found wandering in these parts must be considered fair game.' Mama could hardly make him take it back if he didn't know to whom it belonged. Someone at the pub reported finding a note next to a meatless skeleton that read *You are rich, we are poor. When this has gone, we'll fetch some more!*[5]

"Everyone began to feel the effects of the strike. People were not buying goods in the shops and they weren't hiring trades people to repair their homes. A group of clergy and businessmen formed a committee to help the needy miners, and established the Stanton and Newhall Bread Fund. I remember going to the post office—I even remember the day, August 18—and looking with amazement at the stacks of bread on the tables. Bread was distributed to the crowd that day and the next, and others pitched in as well. The Bridge family disbursed forty stones (a stone is 14 lbs) of bread and the owners of the Shoulder of Mutton pub gave away broth.

"It was becoming increasingly difficult to feed the hundreds of families that were near to starving, though. I remember we lived mostly on potatoes for a while, and Mama got very clever inventing new ways to prepare them so we wouldn't get bored."

Jane nodded knowingly, her expression empathetic.

"I imagine you know about that," Betsy said to her with a smile.

"Oh, yes!" Jane chuckled.

"Well, one day," Betsy continued, "something happened that changed the course of events dramatically. A man appeared in town, a stranger, almost as though he came from nowhere. Then days later, a newspaper article in the *Burton Gazette* extended a challenge to the people of the region to make a food donation to Mr. Tunnicliffe at the post office. If fifty pounds could be raised in a week, the stranger would provide a further thousand pounds of bread and cheese." Betsy paused and nodded at the surprised murmurs this drew from the other young women.

"Within days, this stranger appeared at a gathering called by the local miners' agent. Many of the men had been engaging in a practice called 'fedding.' This involved extracting coal from the surface seams of an area known as Gresley Common. It was illegal, but the property owners turned a blind eye, as they knew the miners needed the few pounds they could make by selling this surface coal. The men halted their work on these makeshift mines and gathered on High Street to hear how the negotiations were proceeding."

"Following several speeches on the progress of talks with the mine owners—or rather the lack of progress—the stranger asked to have a word with the crowd. He was a tall man, with grey hair and a neatly trimmed grey moustache. He wore a tailored suit and silver cufflinks and tiepin. His shoes fascinated us all because frankly, many of us had resorted to going barefoot by this time. Our clothes were mostly hand-me-downs as well, although I must say, my mother always managed to keep us looking clean and tidy."

"The man began by sympathizing with the miners' plight and condemning the mine owners for their greed. Then he announced that he would provide a free meal for one thousand children at the Swadlincote Market Hall the next day at 4:00 p.m. He also offered to sell six pounds of bread and six pounds of cheese to each adult for one shilling. And," Betsy added over the women's murmurs praising the stranger's generosity, "he would give the bread and cheese free to the most deserving cases!"

"Such generosity!" Mavis exclaimed.

"Yes," Betsy agreed. "We were amazed. It was like Jesus himself had appeared. I don't know who was more excited—the children or their parents. News of this travelled throughout the area so by the next day, I would guess that nearly two thousand hungry children turned up for their free meal. It was all handled in a very orderly way, though, and after the stranger said grace, we were given a nice ration of food. Not one child left hungry. There was not enough left over to fill all the requests for the one-shilling packages, but the stranger apologized and said there would be more forthcoming the following week. He also haggled the local shopkeepers into lowering their prices, and many agreed to offer goods at deep discount prices."

Elizabeth looked thoughtful. "This is wonderful, of course," she said, "but it seems strange that a man would appear from nowhere and so selflessly help a group of miners and their families."

"He was surely a charitable man," Mavis said, "doing God's work."

"Or an activist, perhaps," Jane suggested. She looked expectantly at Betsy, who took the silent cue.

"Not everyone in the town trusted the man's motives, either. The local press printed a series of letters that basically questioned whether he was simply trying to prolong the strike by ensuring that the miners and their families were fed. Others disputed this and suggested the doubters were supporters of the mine owners, trying in their own way to cast dispersions on a man whose only goal was to prevent starvation."

"So what happened?" Mavis asked.

"A few days later," Betsy frowned for a thoughtful moment, "on August 28, I believe, the stranger sent a telegram. It said that three thousand pounds of provisions were arriving by rail, with *twenty thousand pounds* to follow." This drew gasps of admiration.

"Others in the region also began to supply free dinners to children, so it seemed this stranger had served as the impetus for the emergence of local heroes—champions. Later the stranger and his team of helpers set up a program whereby those who wished to make donations to feed the poor could purchase tickets from the various shops for prices as low as a penny. The recipients then exchanged the tickets for a meal or supply of food and the shop-keepers could claim their costs back from the funds held by the stranger. It was thought to be a positive arrangement for all."

"How long did that go on?" Elizabeth asked.

"The strike ended October 16. My father and the other miners returned to work without a cut in their wages. To this day the townsfolk remember the efforts of the stranger and there has been much speculation about just who he was, but no one is absolutely certain."

"How mysterious," Jane said.

"What an amazing tale of kindness," claimed Elizabeth, then looked around the table. "Perhaps" said Betsy. "The strike might have ended sooner if food had not been provided. I guess we will never know. Now that we are finished our meal, shall we all retire to the library for coffee?"

* * *

Betsy hoped she would see Rosa that night, but when she got back to her cabin, her bed had been turned down and Rosa was nowhere to be seen. She didn't feel tired, and decided to read in bed for a while; perhaps Rosa would stop by later. She'd read only a few pages of her book when her eyelids grew heavier and heavier, until they closed completely, and Betsy drifted off.

Betsy awoke with a start, images from a vivid dream still imprinted on her mind's eye. A large black bird had circled over her constantly, never diverging from its path, never flying lower or higher. "What is the significance of that?" she wondered aloud, as if speaking would drive away the last dregs of foreboding. *Was there some danger lurking ahead*?

She looked at her watch; it was late, but the inadvertent nap had left her alert, and she didn't want to risk revisiting the frightening dream just yet. *I'll try this again,* she thought, lifting her book and flipping through the pages until she found the one she'd been reading until it had slid off her lap and closed as she slept.

A short time later, there was a light knock at the door. Betsy rose and moved to open it, to find a smiling Rosa. She returned the smile, pleased to see her new friend, and invited her to come in and sit down. "You must be exhausted after such a long day of work," Betsy said.

"Yes, it is very tiring. These new floors they have on this ship don't help, either. They were supposed to be easier on our feet, but to tell the truth, my feet hurt worse than ever. It doesn't help that I have a couple of serious corns, as well."

Betsy laughed. "Thanks something else we have in common, Rosa!" she declared. "Here, look at what I have on my great toe!" Betsy held up her bare foot and indeed, she had a corn about half an inch thick jutting out from her right toe. The two women laughed. "Take off your shoes and rest a while Rosa," pleaded Betsy.

Grateful for the rare moment of respite, Rosa removed her work shoes and sat back with a sigh to relax her weary bones. Being one of the youngest stewardesses, she admitted, she was often given tasks to do that the others found too strenuous. "Some days, I wonder if I'll have the strength to even finish my shift, I'm so tired. Tonight was one of those nights." She had been asked to scrub down the hallways in three sections of the ship because it had rained during the day. It was a particularly arduous task.

"I saw that you were able to make it to the dining room for dinner, Betsy. You must be feeling a bit better. How was the dinner?"

"Oh, it was lovely. The dining room is ever so nice, almost as nice as the first class one. The meal was excellent. I sat with some girls on their way to New York. They got me talking about life back home in Swadlincote and I'm afraid I talked their ears off.

It's interesting, how easy it is to open up to complete strangers on board a ship."

"I try not to get too involved with most passengers," quipped Rosa. "For some reason I feel well... different with you. Its like we could have been sisters or something."

Betsy smiled. "I feel the same about you Rosa".

The two women sat for about an hour, exchanging stories and opinions on a wide range of topics. Rosa talked about her early experiences on board several ships to South America and explained how she had managed finally to get a position with the White Star. "I had to dress in a dowdy fashion to downplay my youth and good looks, as the first times I applied they said I was simply too young and too pretty to be working on board a ship." The two women agreed that this was a very unfair, discriminatory practice.

In turn, Betsy told Rosa what it was like growing up as a coal miner's daughter in a small town in England. She described how the coal dust hung in the air and clung to everything, how the miners toiled hard underground and almost always contracted lung disease in their middle years, and how the sons of the villagers almost always followed in their father's footsteps when choosing employment.

"I don't know what people there will do for work if they ever close those mines down, or if the coal runs out," Betsy said. "The owners of the mines appear to be very prosperous, but the workers are always underpaid, in most cases living paycheque to paycheque. The differences are never more apparent than when the miners are engaged in one of their many strikes. It has been said that the time for the mine owners to eat is when they are hungry. The time for the striking miners to eat is when they have food."

"I guess I should not complain about the small portions of food we are given here on the ship," Rosa replied. "At least I never go to bed on an empty stomach."

Finally Betsy yawned and Rosa remarked, "I am keeping you up, Betsy, and you need your sleep. I need mine as well. I'll go now, and will see you in the morning." She put on her shoes and moved to the door, then paused with her hand on the doorknob as if remembering something. "Betsy, about your next door neighbour—"

Before she could say more, Betsy gasped. "Oh my goodness! I completely forgot. Rosa, I got it, I have her diary here. I meant to give it to you straight out..." she said as she jumped up from the bed, then turned and reached under the mattress. "Here. It will give you the proof that is needed to take this matter up with the police." She turned and held the black book triumphantly out to Rosa.

"Yes, about that, I've heard back from the security officer here aboard ship." Rosa took the book and carefully. "It seems...did you look at it at all?"

"No," Betsy said. "At first I was so nervous about taking it, and then, well, as I said, I felt so ill afterward that I forgot about it."

Rosa nodded, and strangely, smiled. "It seems... well..." She opened the cover and scanned the front page. Her smile widened. "Yes, it's true."

"What?" Betsy pressed. "What does it reveal?"

Rosa read the lines written on the page aloud. "*The Murder of Captain Hayes. A novel by Bernice Vaughn.*" She looked up at Betsy. There was deathly silence for a moment, as they looked each other in the eye. Betsy was the first to begin to giggle. Rosa agreed to slip the diary back into Mrs. Vaughn's room the next morning.

CHAPTER EIGHT:
THE GUESTS AT TABLE 21

May 20: 2012. Day Four of the Sailing

Betsy awoke with a calm stomach, a clearer head, and knees that no longer felt wobbly. Thrilled and grateful to at last be feeling normal, she rose, washed up in the small sink in her room, and after slipping into her corset and tightening the strings, dressed in one of her two long gabardine dresses. Then she sat in front of the mirror and ran the hairbrush through her long, silky brown hair. Not many people even knew that she had hair that fell almost to her waist. As was usually her custom, she divided the hair in two and braided it once more into the two long braids that she wrapped about her head and secured it with tiny pins. Surveying her reflection as she scraped the loose hair off the brush, she declared herself fit to meet the world. Betsy eagerly headed off to have breakfast in the second class dining salon.

A sign posted at the door caught her eye as she arrived: *Table 21 reserved for passengers who originally had passage on the Titanic.* Below the header was a list of names. Betsy scanned the list and was pleased to find she had been included. *What an intriguing idea,* she thought. She had known there must be others aboard the ship who had experienced the same delay and transfer as she, but she had no idea who they were or how they might connect. *Are they experiencing the same feelings of guilt mixed with relief that I have been undergoing?* she wondered. She suspected that similar gatherings were scheduled in the first class and steerage dining room.

She walked around the room until she found Table 21, and took a seat. At first she was all alone, but soon a middle-aged couple joined her.

"Hello, young lady," the tall, silver-haired man said, then tapped his chest. "Frank Wilkinson, and this is my wife Alicia. We're from Virginia. Americans, we are," he announced loudly in a heavy southern accent. "I believe this is the table reserved for those who missed the *Titanic* sailing. That would be us!"

"Good morning to you both," Betsy replied. "Yes, that's what I saw on the poster by the door. I was rather hoping I would meet others who had the same experience I had. Have you sailed across the ocean often?" she asked as they seated themselves across from her at the long table.

"Oh yes," replied Alicia. "We've taken many trips to Europe. On this particular one, we were en route home from India." She glanced at Frank and patted his arm. "My husband is an importer and travels worldwide to seek out goods to bring to America. I love going with him. It gives me a chance to shop abroad for the latest fashions and shoes."

Betsy had noticed her gown as the couple sat down, a lovely, ankle-length maroon dress that clearly came from a London or Paris fashion house. *I wonder why they chose to sail second class instead of first?* she thought. *They appear to be quite well off.*

Moments later two teenage boys joined the table. They introduced themselves as Charles and Henry Clarkson, brothers who hailed from London. "We are en route to Chicago to join our parents," explained Charles, the elder of the two. Betsy smiled and admired his fresh young freckled face and sparkling green eyes. Henry, his junior, had the same green eyes with dimples instead of freckles.

Before they could continue a slender, handsome man who looked to be in his mid-twenties arrived. He spoke with a thick French accent and sported a rather formal smoking jacket. He shook hands around the table and introduced himself. "Pierre Leblanc from Paris. I am going to Canada to work as an agent for the Hudson Bay Company."

Betsy was intrigued and pulled a tiny wisp of her hair loose, twirling it between her fingers. She felt her cheeks flush. Mr. Leblanc was quite charming. "I'm going to Canada as well. Where will you be staying?" she asked.

"I'm heading for Winnipeg. From there I'll be covering an area in Northern Manitoba. They tell me it is quite cold there, a place where temperatures rarely rise over minus twenty degrees Fahrenheit in the long winter." Betsy placed the strand of hair back behind her ear and leaned back in her chair.

The last passengers joined the table, introducing themselves as Dr. J. Stewart, Miss Anne Burns, and finally Reverend J. Stuart Holbrook. Since their numbers now exceeded the eight places set at the table, the steward quickly brought another place setting and a chair for the final table guest. The extra setting brought the tablemates closer together so that in some cases, they barely had elbowroom to enjoy their meal. But no one seemed upset by this, and there was an air of anticipation as coffee was served to each guest.

Betsy was fascinated by the sense of immediate camaraderie at Table 21, the kind of familiarity that she would have expected if she attended a family reunion and met a crowd of people for the first time who were all related, albeit in some distant fashion.

Frank Wilkinson opened up the conversation, addressing the entire table. "We must be among the luckiest people alive in the world. I don't know how you folks managed to miss the sailing of the *Titanic*, but my wife and I were on our way home from India. We had booked our passage months in advance but at the last minute, a great business opportunity came up for me in Bombay. We missed our intended vessel travelling to England and had to reschedule. At that point they informed us that our passage on the maiden *Titanic* voyage to America would need to be changed as well. I must say we were dreadfully disappointed, but I can tell you that later events removed all that. How about the rest of you?"

The two teenage boys grinned sheepishly. For a moment neither spoke. Then Charles began. "Our folks have already moved to Chicago, where my father is teaching university. We were to sail on the *Titanic* to meet them after first spending a few days in Southampton. We were so excited to be going on its maiden voyage."

The younger boy spoke next. "We were staying in a small inn on Victoria Street. We had one of six rooms located over top of the neighbourhood drinking establishment—the Pickled Pig's Toe. We'd made friends with some of the local lads in the pub and on the night before the sailing, they proceeded to give us a royal send-off. It consisted of a grand tour of all of the pubs in the area, of course with a pint or two at each."

Charles interrupted his brother. "I am not sure at what point I realized we were missing Henry. I think it was about two in the morning. I remember feeling panicky and asking all the lads what had become of him. No one could remember for sure when they last saw him. We decided to retrace our steps at all of the pubs we had been to."

"And a few more beers were consumed, I imagine," Frank Wilkinson interrupted with a chuckle.

Charles blushed and nodded, looking sideways at the Reverend to see if he wore a disapproving look. Betsy followed his gaze and saw the sparkle in the man's eye and the smile on his lips. "I can tell you," Charles finished, "I have never been that drunk before, nor will I be again."

Henry took up the story. "Unbeknownst to the others, I had gone searching for a toilet. Somehow, I ended up in an alleyway out back of the pub. My head was spinning and I decided to sit down for a few minutes—but I fell asleep! The next sound I heard was a couple of hungry dogs rummaging through the garbage that was heaped in the lane. The sun was already up, and I had no idea where I was. After several hours spent wandering, I made my way back to our lodgings, thanks to directions from a few kind strangers."

"Charles and the other blokes were waiting for me when I arrived. Unfortunately—or fortunately, as it turned out—we did not have time to make it to the ship before it departed. I expect our parents were livid when we wired them a telegram telling them we missed the sailing, and would rebook."

Anne, who was seated next to Henry, commented, "It is so fascinating, how a single twist of fate can change the direction of one's life forever. If you boys had been on the ship, you would have no doubt been among the casualties. I understand they rescued mainly women and children—and the first class men, of course."

"We have considered this over and over as well," said Charles. "How about you, Betsy? What prevented you from sailing on that fateful vessel?"

Betsy told them she had signed up for the voyage very late, and had not realized that it would take more time to process her immigration application. "I too was terribly disappointed at the news that I wouldn't be going on the maiden voyage of that great ship," she said. "Everyone was so excited about it. The British press made such a fuss about it being the world's largest passenger ship, and the fact that it was so seaworthy. In hindsight, I have wondered if the sinking would have caused so big a stir, had the press not made such a spectacle of it in the beginning." The others at the table nodded.

Anne Burns leaned forward. "I was all set to travel, but two days before, I developed a fever, nausea, and severe pain in my right lower abdomen. A doctor examined me and at first he thought I had a case of influenza. However, the next day my fever continued to rise and the pain became excruciating. I was rushed to hospital and diagnosed as having appendicitis. After the surgery I remained in hospital for a week. I was so disappointed about missing the sailing, but like all of you, I later felt overwhelmingly blessed. It has had a profound effect on me somehow. My life had been lacking in purpose up till then but I actually feel obligated to do something very worthwhile now. I was given a second chance. I want to make it meaningful." She looked around the table. "Does anyone else feel that way?"

Dr. Stewart nodded. "Yes, I feel that responsibility as well. You know, you were very lucky that you didn't get on board the ship and then get sick. They have a surgeon on board, but frankly, I don't know how much practice he gets. If it were me, I would be reluctant to let him start cutting me up."

Everyone nodded. Betsy had been thinking of going to the ship's doctor for her seasickness, but now she was a little relieved that she hadn't. *But surely they would know about treating seasickness,* she mused.

Dr. Stewart shifted back to the topic of the *Titanic*. "I am heading off to the American Midwest to take over a medical practice set up by my uncle. He is becoming quite frail and can't tolerate the long hours. Apparently he is the only doctor for many miles around. At any rate, I was all set to leave for Southampton when there was an outbreak of typhoid fever in my rather rundown district of south Glasgow. Not only was I needed there to treat the sick, but I was placed in quarantine for three weeks, so I had to rebook my passage. Fortunately I did not succumb to the disease myself, but in my district alone there were over twenty-five deaths attributed to the horrid disease. Most of those were elderly people or those with asthma or chronic bronchitis."

Only Norman Craig and Reverend Holbrook had yet to tell their stories when the steward came with the hot porridge. "Let's wait to hear from the rest of you after we eat. We don't want our food to get cold," suggested Frank Wilkinson. The guests all nodded in agreement.

Betsy was surprised to find that her appetite had returned in full force, and she was amazed at how good everything tasted. "This Edwardian breakfast is fit for a king," Norman Craig declared, and then added in response to several blank looks from his tablemates, "King Edward VII set a good example for us all. He apparently began his days with haddock, grilled steaks, chops, or cutlets, and poached eggs. This was topped up with spit-roasted chickens and woodcock."

"Sounds like our late king was quite the carnivore," Betsy noted with a small smile. "We are so lucky to be fed so well here."

"Even the third class meals on this ship are apparently quite good," Reverend Holbrook said. "Apparently until recently, they were expected to bring their own food on board the ship. But one of my parishioners recently travelled back from

New York on this ship in the steerage section and described having a breakfast of oatmeal porridge, smoked herring, jacket potatoes, tripe, and onions." The Reverend paused and allowed a small frown. "But he said the biscuits were very hard and lacking in flavour." Betsy chuckled with the others.

Most of the guests finished their meal with hot coffee, which was when the original conversation picked up where it had left off. Norman Craig began. "I too fell ill just before the *Titanic* sailed. Mine was a case of pneumonia I picked up during a particularly cold blizzard in my native northern Wales. But my strong constitution helped me recover quickly—just not in time for the grand *Titanic* send-off." This brought a few chuckles, but then his voice grew pensive. "In truth, I don't know why I was spared while other more deserving men lost their lives that fateful night. I too have wondered if maybe God has some other plan in store for me, something else I need to accomplish before being called away to His side."

Reverend Holbrook smiled. "I could not have said it better myself, son. I believe that is the case for all of us here. There is a reason why we were spared, even if we don't know it now. In fact, we may never know the reason. But I suspect each of us will, in our own way, make some kind of mark on the world. Or maybe one of our sons, daughters, grandchildren, or greatgrandchildren will."

And then he shared with the group why he'd failed to use his ticket on the *Titanic*. It was beyond all doubt the saddest story that Betsy had heard from any of those at Table 21. "I was ready to come to America, had my bags packed, had my ticket, and I was excited about taking up a parish in rural New England. I gave a sermon on the last Sunday before the departure and at the end, when we gave out the communion at the altar, a young man of about twenty-one slouched over and began sobbing. I quietly asked him if I could pray for him and when he said yes, I placed my hand on his head, and asked God to grant him peace of mind in terms of what was troubling him. It calmed him."

"After the service, he came over to tell me why he was so distraught. His mother, who was living in California, had suddenly taken very ill. She had no other relatives nearby. The young man and his sister had taken over their father's greengrocer business in England when their parents decided to retire and live in the United States. His father died soon after they arrived there, and while the mother wanted to return to England, she did not feel strong enough to make the trip alone. She was waiting for one of her children to come and escort her back."

"Well, there I was standing with a ticket to New York in my pocket. There was only one thing to do. I reached into my pocket and handed the ticket to the young man. Tears of joy welled up in his eyes and he thanked me over and over."

Mrs. Wilkinson was the first to break the silence that followed. "That was an amazingly unselfish act of kindness on your part," she said quietly. "I hope it turned out okay for the boy in the end."

The Reverend sighed. "Actually, it didn't, I'm afraid. He was not on the list of survivors. I 've been carrying around a great burden of guilt ever since." The pastor's eyes glittered with tears. "Oh, I know God doesn't blame me, but the lad was so young!" he choked out. "He had so much life to live." He paused for a moment to calm himself, and when he spoke again his voice was more matter-of-fact, as if turning to business would keep his emotions at bay. "I followed up to see how his death would be handled by the shipping company. The White Star Line offered to have his sister go over to get their mother, at their expense. I believe that is what she is planning to do. I'm sure there will be insurance money offered to the family as well."

"That must have been difficult for you," Anne Burns said gently. "I too have had feelings of guilt, but you will have this on your conscience for a long time. I hope you can make peace with yourself."

That brought another thoughtful silence to the group. Finally Charles stood, and Henry rose beside him, shifting from one foot to the other uncomfortably. They looked around the table, flashing brief smiles, and Charles announced, "It's been lovely to meet everyone. We'll be off now, but we'll surely see some of you about the ship."

On that note, the members of the group rose and proceeded out of the dining hall. Betsy found Anne Burns walking beside her and asked her what she had planned for the day. "I have decided to pamper myself today," Anne declared. "I'm going to have a Turkish sauna and a dip in the pool. After that I'll have a massage from one of the Turkish bath attendants. I'm feeling rather stiff and tense and haven't had much exercise since leaving home. I'm ready for a day of relaxation."

"Oh, that sounds heavenly," remarked Betsy.

"And you?" Anne asked. "What are your plans?"

"I think I will take a stroll on the deck and get some fresh air. I was seasick for the first few days and spent them cooped up in my cabin. After that I will likely look for a good book in the library."

"So we will both be relaxing in our own way," Anne said, her tone approving. "Shall we meet for dinner and compare our days?"

"That sound lovely," Betsy said, happy to have a companion at dinner. "I'll see you then."

"Wonderful," Anne said, then lifted her hand in a little wave as she moved away, calling back, "And have a pleasant day!"

CHAPTER NINE:
THE ONE ABOUT
THE BLUE DRESS

Later Day 4

Betsy wandered out onto the promenade and stood at the rail, looking out at the vast ocean. After the conversation at breakfast, she couldn't help shuddering at the thought of being in the middle of that ocean in a lifeboat, alone but for other struggling passengers, fighting hypothermia and fear. She was relieved when she turned and found Rosa standing by her side.

"Good morning, Betsy. You look one hundred percent better today. How are you feeling?" she asked.

"So much better," Betsy replied, meaning that in more ways than one. But she knew what Rosa meant. "I'm finally getting what they call my sea legs, I guess." The two women laughed. "I even enjoyed an amazing breakfast with a group of very interesting people. I must tell you all about it."

"Oh yes, I would enjoy that," Rosa said. "But I came looking for you for a specific reason. Do you think you could spare a couple of hours to give me a hand over in the gymnasium, where the children are gathered from first and second class? We have quite a few youngsters there today. So far, all of the children on board have entertained themselves playing deck quoits and shuffleboard, and running and skipping games on the deck. Now, though, I am running out of ideas of how to entertain them. You have such great experience as a governess. I thought you might be willing to help me out."

"What is deck quoits?" asked Betsy. "I've not heard of that."

"Deck quoits is popular on cruise ships. It's like the original game of the same name that is played in neighbourhood pubs in Britain, except the quoits on a ship are made of rope so they won't damage the ship's deck. I don't think there are any universally agreed standards or rules—it's an informal game that is adapted to the area of each particular ship it is played upon. Players take turns throwing three or four hoops at a target, which is usually three concentric circles marked on the deck. The centre point, which is called the jack, is sometimes a raised wooden peg, but here on the *Olympic* it is simply marked on the deck the same way that the concentric circles are.

Would you like to see where quoits are played? There will likely be a game in process, so you'll be able to see what I mean."

"Is it on the way to the gymnasium?" Betsy asked and when Rosa nodded, she said, "Then let's go entertain those children!"

Rosa smiled. "Oh I am so glad you will give me a hand."

After getting a quick demonstration of deck quoits by some obliging players, Betsy followed Rosa into the gymnasium. Half a dozen girls aged about four through seven, all clad in the latest children's fashions, came running eagerly up to them. "Can you tell us a story?" one of the girls pleaded, and the others echoed, "A story! Yes, a story—please tell us a story!"

Rosa looked at Betsy, who smiled and nodded to her, indicating that she was in her element. Indeed, Betsy had spent many hours telling Marjory Turnball stories, and she knew just which one she would start with.

Thank you, Rosa mouthed, and backed away to approach another group of youngsters.

Betsy looked around at her young audience. "Alright," she said, "let's sit down. I think I have just the story."

One little girl with blonde ringlets took her right hand, and another girl with a brown bob took her left, and giggling, the gaggle of little girls guided Betsy over to a small table. When they were all settled, Betsy looked around at their upturned faces and asked, "How would you like to hear..." she dropped her voice as if the story were a special secret "...the one about the blue dress? It's a true story."

This met a chorus of oohs and "Yes! Tell us that one!" And so she began.

"It was a warm, muggy afternoon on June 13, 1888."

"That's a long time ago," one girl observed solemnly.

"Betsy smiled. "Yes, it was."

"Are the people in the story old?" asked another.

"Oh, no," Betsy said. "Elizabeth was only six, small and thin, and her sister, Sarah Ann, was not too much older. However—" she paused dramatically, and the little girls leaned forward, eyes wide, waiting for Betsy's next pronouncement "—on this day, as they walked past the Newhall mine pit on their way home from school, Elizabeth moved more like she was eighty years old, not at all like the perky little girl her Alma Road neighbours had grown accustomed to. Her head hung low, and her eyes were downcast."

One of the little girls gasped. "What was wrong?" Several nodded, turning concerned eyes back to Betsy.

"As they entered the front hall of their row house, their mother, Jane, wondered that too, when she noticed Elizabeth's downcast face. Hoping to cheer her daughter up, she said she had just made a special something for the afternoon tea."

"What was it?" the girl with blonde ringlets asked.

"Freshly baked scones," Betsy told her. "But Elizabeth was in no mood for tea. Even the smell of freshly baked scones didn't take away her dark mood. She headed straight up the stairs to the tiny room that she shared with her sister.

"Elizabeth's Mother fixed up a nice tea tray and quietly ascended the staircase and entered her daughters' bedroom. 'Whatever is the matter?' she asked as she set the tea tray on the bed. 'You look like your best friend just died!'"

Another gasp. "She didn't, did she?" the little girl with the brown bob exclaimed.

"Oh no, that would be sad. This isn't a sad story, is it?" asked the girl beside her.

"Well, at the time, Elizabeth thought it was," said Betsy. "She was rolled up in a little ball on her bed, but her mother could see she was crying. 'Whatever is the matter, my dear?' Jane asked gently."

"'Oh Mommy!' Elizabeth finally blurted out. 'All the girls in my class will be singing in the school concert tonight except me. It's horrible! I asked you months ago if I could have a pretty dress like the others and sing the lullaby song with my dolly. I know you told me there was barely enough money for food, let alone a new dress. But it's dreadful and it's not fair. I shan't be able to face any of them tomorrow, when they will all be chatting and bragging about the wonderful time they had. Leave me alone,' Elizabeth sobbed. 'I wish I was dead.'

"Jane sat down on the edge of the bed. Her heart was aching for her little one, but she had to be strong. That was what her mother had taught her. She peered at Elizabeth over the brim of her wire-framed glasses and said firmly, 'Elizabeth, all the crying in the world is not going to change things. Your pa has been short of work now for over two months because of a slow-down in the mines, and yet we always have food on the table and coal for the hearth at night. You should not be so selfish and ungrateful, to be mourning the lack of a frilly new gown for a concert. There will be many more concerts in your life.'

"'But Mama,' whined Elizabeth, 'I even offered to sweep the floor every day if you would buy some blue silk and make me a dress. All the girls are wearing blue silk dresses and I will never, never have a chance to sing again in this concert. It's so unfair. Take away the tea. Just leave me alone.'

"On this note, Jane, troubled by her daughter's distress, picked up the tea tray and headed wearily downstairs to the kitchen, where Sara was diving into her third scone, having piled it high with butter and fresh preserves. 'Sara, you are only nine years old,' Jane scolded. 'You'll soon be needing a corset if you keep that up. Proper girls don't normally need to be corseted until they are thirteen. And leave some scones for your pa. He'll be home soon and he will be famished.'

"She paused, cleaning her glasses on her apron. 'I am at my wits end with your sister,' she sighed. 'I wish I could have found the money to get her material for a dress for the concert tonight. We must all go down to the school at 6:30 in order to get good seats. It will be dreadful for her, but she must learn that life isn't always fair.'

"When tea time was over and Watty, Elizabeth's pa, was seated in his chair with his pipe, Jane and Sara Ann headed upstairs to get ready to go to the school concert. Just at that moment there was knock at the door. Watty rose and shuffled over to answer it. His back ached from a hard day in the mine, because even with the horses to haul the load up, he had done more than his share of lifting."

"At the door stood Cora Tunnicliff, the cheerful teenage daughter of the Newhall sub-postmaster, who lived at Number 12 Alma Road. 'My mama asked me come and get Elizabeth,' she said. 'We would like her to come with us to the concert tonight.'

"Watty sighed. While child rearing was normally Jane's domain, she had told him about the saga of the concert. It had only made him feel worse about the small amount of money he earned at the mine. 'I will go and see if she is ready,' he muttered. He climbed the stairs wearily and tapped on the girls' bedroom door. 'Elizabeth, come downstairs. Cora from up the street is here. She and her mother want you to walk over to the concert with them.'

'I'm not going.' Elizabeth called out. 'I shall stay in my room tonight, tomorrow, and forever rather than face all those girls. They are wicked and mean, Papa, and they won't forget about this ever.'

"For all of his gruffness, Watty was not an unkind man. He strode into the room and scooped his young daughter up in his arms. 'Elizabeth, my little plum pudding, I think you should wipe away those tears. You are an Oakes girl, and Oakes girls are not so easily provoked. Your Grandma Oakes was as strong as an ox and put up with all kinds of hardship. And your mother's mother, Grandma Eagles, practically ran the greengrocers single-handedly over in Wedsbury.'

"He wiped her long, blonde tresses away from her eyes. She struggled, but only ever so briefly, and by the time he had carried her down the stairs to the front door, she had regained her composure. She stepped outside with Cora. The air was crisp and damp and Elizabeth hoped Sara would remember to wear a sweater, as she seemed to suffer from cold after cold in the damp weather."

"I do too," one of the little listeners said solemnly, and shuddered for effect.

Betsy smiled at her before continuing her story. "When they got to Cora's house, Mrs. Tunnicliff, a tall, willowy woman in her early forties, greeted them. Her hands were gnarled from working in the garden, raising enough produce to feed her own small family and nearly half the other residents of Alma Road, during the lean years. 'Why, good afternoon, Miss Oakes" she said, smiling and taking Elizabeth's hand. 'I have a surprise for you, but you must promise to tell no one before the concert. Come with me into the back room.'

"Elizabeth was perplexed. Mrs. Tunnicliffe was known to be the most generous person on the whole street. But this sort of individual attention from her was something quite new."

Another of the children interrupted Betsy. "Oh, I feel so bad for young Elizabeth. Why would they make her go to the concert? It would only add to the hurt she felt. If it was me I wouldn't go either."

Betsy put her arm around the young passenger. "Wait, my dear, and hear what happened," she said, and continued her story.

"As they entered the back room, Elizabeth gasped. 'Oh my!' she said. 'I have never seen anything so beautiful in all my life!'

"What?" one of the little listeners exclaimed. "What did she see?"

"Well," Betsy said, looking around at their faces, "there on a chair hung the most lovely blue satin dress in the world. It was meticulously hand sewn, with lace collar and puffy sleeves, and beside it hung a long, blue satin sash for tying up Elizabeth's long auburn hair. Elizabeth could not believe her eyes. She was stunned. 'Whoever is this for?' she asked."

"'I found the material on sale down at Robinson's general store on High Street,' Mrs. Tunnicliffe said. 'I knew you needed a blue dress, Elizabeth, and so I made it just for you. Quickly—slip off your clothes and try it on.'

"Elizabeth gingerly obeyed, still in a state of shock over her neighbour's unexpected kindness. When the dress was on, Mrs. Tunnicliffe gently brushed her hair back and tied the beautiful blue ribbon around it with a large bow on top. 'There now,' said Mrs. Tunnicliffe. 'You look absolutely stunning. Shall we leave to go to the concert?'

"Elizabeth twirled around once, just to see how far the satin would spread and to feel it tingling against her legs. 'Oh yes!' she exclaimed. 'But I am missing one thing. We are supposed to bring our dollies with us.'

'Not to worry,' said Mrs. Tunnicliffe. 'I have your dolly here already. I got Cora to ask your mother for it this morning.' She left and returned to the room and to Elizabeth's utter surprise she saw that her precious doll was clad in an identical blue satin gown. Tears welled up in her eyes. Never in her life had she dreamed of owning such a beautiful frock."

"The trio headed to the concert at the small public school down the road. When they arrived, Elizabeth joined the other girls in her classroom, who were all parading around in their finery. The teacher, Miss Woodville, was having a hard time settling them and was looking forward to the end of the night, and the end of the school year, so she could return to her native London for a rest. The girls gasped with amazement and a little envy when they saw Elizabeth and her identically clad dolly."

"The lights went down in the auditorium. Everyone hushed as the headmaster announced the first act of the concert: the Grade One class. Elizabeth fell into line with her fellow students and slowly walked up the aisle and onto the stage. Miss Woodville sat down at the piano, the spotlight was turned on, and the sweet voices of twenty-five young princesses began the strains of "Rock-a-bye Baby," each holding her doll in her arms."

"'Oh, they are lovely,' whispered Jane to her daughter Sara, seated by her side. 'I feel so bad for poor Elizabeth.' But as her eyes moved across the stage, she sucked in her breath. There in the centre of the front row was a vision so lovely, that she had to close her eyes and look again. Indeed, it was her very own Elizabeth, smiling and singing and rocking her doll. She imagined she saw a halo behind this beautiful creature, who only six years before had been a colicky, crying baby."

"Elizabeth began to sing shyly, but as she saw the grins and smiles of encouragement from the parents and friends in the audience, she found her powerful voice and by the time the song ended, she knew that this miracle proved that no matter how rough times may seem, there really is a God. Or at the very least, an amazingly kind neighbour."

"No one in the audience ever forgot that concert, least of all Betsy, who recounted it to the children on board the *Olympic* several times. "Miss Betsy," they would say, "tell us the one about the blue dress again." And she did. She decided to withhold the fact that this story was her story.

As the storytelling session ended, a group of boys came over and suggested a game of quoits. Relieved that she'd had a demonstration earlier, Betsy gathered the boys together and explained the rules to those who were unfamiliar with the game. Each boy took his turn and the game went well until they began roughhousing, then Betsy had to step in and grasp two of the boys who were pushing each other about more and more aggressively by the collar to restrain them.

"Take your hands off of me," demanded one of the boys.

Betsy let go of the two lads, but not before reprimanding them severely. As they skulked away, she scanned the area in search of Rosa to ask her how they normally handled discipline on board the ship, but Rosa had slipped out of the gymnasium and was nowhere in sight. *That's strange,* she thought. *I didn't know she was leaving me in charge of the place. I wonder where she has disappeared to.* She continued the game with the boys, keeping a more watchful eye out for the safety of rest of the children playing in the gymnasium.

After about an hour, Rosa returned. She looked a little flushed and her eyes were red. Betsy lifted an eyebrow but didn't say anything, deciding it was best not to pry, although she did wish the stewardess had alerted her to the fact that she was going to be left alone with all of those children. *If it's important, Rosa will surely tell me why she had to leave me alone here,* she told herself, and walked over to help Rosa and the children put away all of the playthings. When the children were gone, she and Rosa had a chance to chat.

"I have met the most interesting people on board this ship, Rosa," Betsy said as she tossed a stray ball into its storage basket. "A table was set up at breakfast today for people who were originally booked on the *Titanic* and had been unable to make the voyage for some reason. Remember I told you that I was supposed to sail on her maiden voyage, but my immigration papers were not ready in time? It was so interesting, hearing the others' stories of how they missed that fateful sailing."

"Betsy, that was so lucky for you." Rosa lowered her eyes, then looked up, as if deciding something. She slowly breathed out. "I haven't told you something. I was", she paused, "I was actually on the

Titanic the night that it sank. In fact, this is my first voyage since being rescued. I was advised not to discuss this with any of the passengers, but somehow I just feel I can open up to you in a personal way. You have been so open with me."

"Oh, my word!" exclaimed Betsy. "That must have been a very traumatic experience for you. You must still be in shock! I wish we had more time to talk but I need to go and prepare for dinner now. I can hardly wait to hear your experience. You must tell me all about it later." *In fact I need a bit of time to absorb what I just heard* thought Betsy, her mind reeling.

As they parted, both women sensed that more layers of their respective souls would be unveiled in the few remaining days ahead. Both were hopeful that what they revealed would be accepted with kindness and warmth and without judgement.

CHAPTER TEN:
TWISTS OF FATE

Betsy returned to her stateroom, eager for her next meeting with Rosa. She had been shocked by the young stewardess's revelation. In the meantime, she thought about the wonderful and inquisitive children she'd met in the gymnasium that day. They seemed so self-confident and outgoing compared to the quieter, more reserved child she had been in charge of for nearly ten years.

How would she go about raising her own, if ever she were given the chance? What was the best discipline to use to ensure that they were infused with high moral standards and proper etiquette? Her humble upbringing as a coal miner's daughter had not provided her with all of the knowledge she needed to instil a more refined set of values in youngsters—that, she'd had to learn along the way in her work as a servant. But learn it she had, and she had never felt more ready to exercise her maternal instincts than at that moment. *All I need is a husband to get started,* she mused. *Best I get up and start moving—he's unlikely to show up in my stateroom here!*

She laughed to herself and rose from the bed where she'd been resting to sit at the desk. She had just enough time before dinner to write a note to her father. Lifting a pen, she pulled one of the silk post-cards with the *Olympic* pictured on the front from the drawer, and wrote on the back:

> *May 21, 1912*
>
> *Dearest Father,*
>
> *Sorry not to have written sooner but due to rough seas and my complete lack of ocean-going experience, I have been laid up with seasickness for most of the trip so far. Am feeling better today so hope it's over. I miss you. Have met a lovely stewardess who has taken great care of me so all is not bad. The ship is wonderful. More later.*
>
> *Your loving Betsy*

She carefully capped the fountain pen and set it down. It was time to meet Anne Burns for dinner. They'd agreed to meet at Table 21 again.

The pianist was playing Beethoven's Moonlight Sonata as she entered the dining saloon, and she was pleased that she recognized the piece. She had never heard Classical music before her employment with the Turnballs. They were not very familiar with Classical music either, but it was well known that if you were to succeed in the middle class, you had to cultivate good taste in music, art, and other finer things in life. So Betsy had been charged with selecting good music to play on the gramophone for Margery in the nursery and in the library for the family after dinner. She had grown particularly fond of Beethoven and Mozart, but in no way would she consider herself to be an expert in Classical music.

Betsy found most of the morning's breakfast guests already seated at Table 21 when she approached. This had instantly become "their table," she realized. It had been so interesting hearing their stories that morning that Betsy could not wait to follow up on the conversation. She seated herself next to Anne Burns, the lovely black-haired young woman from the southern coast of England.

"How was your day at the spa?" she inquired, noting that Anne had a relaxed look about her and a glow to her complexion.

"Absolutely wonderful. I loved the Turkish bath; it was so calming, and it opened up all my pores. Which made the dip in the pool exhilarating, I must say!" Anne chuckled. "They could stand to heat up the water—it was frightfully cold. But it did the trick, and closed up those open pores from the sauna."

"Oh, I wish I had been feeling well enough to join you, Anne," Betsy said. "I am just getting over three horrid days of seasickness, so I don't want to push myself just yet. How was the massage?"

"Oh, it was really great," Anne sighed. "The attendant I had was Swedish and specialized in a type of massage they practise in that country. He had large, strong hands and I felt like every muscle in my body was worked over. He used a type of eucalyptus oil that worked its way through my nasal passages, opening them to let in full blasts of air with each breath." Anne leaned toward Betsy and dropped her voice, although she was grinning conspiratorially. "I was so relaxed at the end that I dropped off to sleep! He left me that way for about half an hour, and then gently woke me up. I don't know that I have ever felt so pampered. It was exactly what I needed. After all my troubles with appendicitis and surgery, I deserved to feel like a queen for a day, don't you think?"

Betsy agreed, and turned to welcome Dr. Stewart, who sat down on her right. They exchanged pleasantries and he asked how she had passed the day. Betsy described her afternoon in the gymnasium with the children. When she mentioned playing quoits, Dr. Stewart exclaimed, "Fancy that. That's a game we play in the pubs in Scotland. There it is done with metal rings and a pegboard on the wall. There is a similar game called horseshoes that is played out of doors. I'll bet the children enjoyed quoits. They must get so restless, being cooped up on this ship for days on end."

"Yes," Betsy replied. "I had to settle down two boys who got carried away with roughhousing, but overall, they are adept at being able to find things to amuse themselves. The ship has a number of games and they were great about sharing their toys from home with each other."

Betsy was regaining her appetite and could not wait for the evening meal to commence. Once most of the guests were seated, the stewards began serving the first course of crème of leek and potato soup. It was one of Betsy's favourites and one that she'd often requested of the cook at the Turnballs'.

She carefully dipped her spoon in the bowl away from her and brought the spoon up to her lips in the manner she understood to be proper. Only the two lads, Charles and Henry Clarkson, failed to eat their soup in the same careful way. Henry finished up by lifting his bowl to drink the last bit. No one said anything, but knowing looks were exchanged all around.

The next course was a choice of duck confit with blueberry sauce, roast pork with applesauce, or sole with almonds. A broad assortment of vegetables arrived as well, and a brief hush fell over the room as the hungry passengers tucked into their main course.

"Its amazing what good appetites we have, considering the little exercise we get here on this ship," remarked Norman Craig. Betsy took note of his rather portly constitution and made a silent vow to herself to try to get more activity into her life, once she was settled in Canada. She was feeling that her corset had gotten a little tighter, especially around her breasts and hips. *Amazing in spite of my poor appetite,* she thought. *If I keep gaining weight I'll lower my chances of attracting a nice husband even more".*

Following the meal, when dessert had been served, Reverend Holbrook decided to talk more about the impact that missing the *Titanic* had had on him. "I have barely been able to sleep a wink since hearing the news of the sinking of that great ship. I get into bed and my mind starts to generate a host of unanswerable questions. What if I had not given away my ticket? What if my offer had been refused? If I'd been on the ship, would I have been ordered into one of the lifeboats? Not likely, I imagine. And so it continues. I feel haunted and yet at the same time I feel blessed. It is hard to explain. Particularly to someone who has not had this experience."

"I know exactly what you mean, Reverend," Mrs. Wilkinson said. "We stayed behind in Bombay to do some extra business. The deal my husband landed there is apt to net us over $20,000 in profit. I said to him this morning that we should plan to do something charitable with that money. It doesn't feel like it belongs to us."

Mr. Wilkinson shifted uncomfortably and cleared his throat. "Well, I agree we were most lucky, dear, but let's not go too far in giving away our profits. We still have to finance our travel costs and there are always more expenses associated with doing the kind of business that we do. I will give some thought to making a donation to our local church when we get home. If we get home."

Everyone fell silent. It was as if he had read their thoughts and the fears that were hovering beneath their consciousness. If the *Titanic* sank, and these ships were identical, who was to say that this ship too could not endure the same fate?

"Thank you for bringing this out in the open, Mr. Wilkinson. I think all of us and many of the other passengers on the ship are wondering the same thing!" exclaimed Anne Burns. "I know I have been wondering just how far they went in improving this ship after the sinking. I tried to find out, but so far I have only gotten rather vague answers."

"Well, I have been told by one of the stewardesses that this ship is being taken out of action for about six months to undergo a complete refitting of some of the underbelly," claimed Betsy. "But until then, I guess it still does have some of the design flaws of the *Titanic*. Not a very comforting thought, is it?"

The conversation turned to speculation about why the *Titanic* sank. There were so many theories that there was no shortage of participation—each guest had heard of a somewhat different explanation. It seemed that most of the current arguments centered on a combination of human error, mechanical failure, and just plain bad luck.

"We all know that the ship collided with an iceberg and sustained a severe crack, which led to the sinking. That is not in dispute. But why did it happen? Was it preventable? That's what is on everyone's mind now," Mr. Wilkinson said.

"It was Captain Smith's retirement trip," Dr. Stewart said. "Maybe he was past his prime and exercised bad judgment in handling the ship that night. I heard that he ignored as many as seven iceberg warnings from his crew and other ships in an attempt to get to New York in record time. If he had called for the ship to slow down, maybe the disaster would not have happened."

Everyone nodded. "Makes sense," Mr. Wilkinson said.

Everyone agreed, that is, except Charles Clarkson. "But I have heard that Captain Smith was the most expert and seasoned captain in the world. It doesn't make sense to me that he would not heed such warnings and take appropriate preventive action. That's one thing my parents have taught us—have respect for your elders. They carry a lot of wisdom and experience that we young people lack. If any of the crew was at fault, I would be willing to bet that it wasn't Captain Smith." Several appreciative smiles were sent his way, particularly from the older guests at the table.

"Good point, son," said Norman Craig. "In support of your theory, it has been reported that the radio operator was so busy sending messages home for passengers that he actually ignored some of the radio warnings that came in. In fact, he asked one radio operator to 'shut up' as he was very busy. I have also heard that Bruce Ismay, Managing Director of the White Star Line, was on board the *Titanic* and may have put pressure on Smith to travel more quickly than was safe, to prove to the world that his company had not only the most luxurious ships, but also the fastest."

"That theory certainly makes some sense," Dr. Stewart said. "There is also speculation that this was the shipbuilder's fault, or at least an error on the part of the architect, Mr. Andrews. The *Titanic* had sixteen watertight compartments that apparently did not reach as high as they should have. People have speculated that the White Star Line did not want them to go all the way up because this would have reduced living space in first class. If Mr. Andrews had insisted on making them the correct height, then maybe the *Titanic* would not have sunk."

"At the same time, there was a shortage of good steel available when the ship was being assembled," Reverend Holbrook added. "Someone speculated that perhaps they used substandard rivets in the construction of the hull. I guess that will never be known, as I understand the *Titanic* sank so deep that she will never be seen again."

He hesitated, and then went on. "As much as I hate to admit this as a possibility, there are some who are putting forth an alternative conspiracy theory. It concerns the Federal Reserve Bank, a Jesuit establishment which some believe is being created so that the order will be able to loan money, shape the world landscape, and become one of the most powerful organizations in the world. It turns out that just two years ago, seven men met on Jekyll Island just off the coast of Georgia to plan the Federal Reserve Bank. Nelson Aldrich and Frank Vanderclip represented the Rockefeller financial empire. Henry Davidson, Charles Norton, and Benjamin Strong represented J.P. Morgan. Paul Warburg represented the Rothschilds Banking dynasty of Europe. The Rothschilds are the banking agents for the Jesuits and hold the key to the wealth of the Roman Catholic Church."[6]

Pierre Leblanc lifted an expressive eyebrow and Dr. Stewart frowned. "And how is this related to the sinking of the *Titanic*?"

"There is apparently some opposition to this master plan from those who think there is danger in having banking outside of the government's hands, with the rates set by a private company such as the Federal Reserve," Reverend Holbrook replied. "As it turns out, all the wealthy and powerful men the

Jesuits wanted to get rid of were invited to take the cruise, including Benjamin Guggenheim, Isador Strauss, the head of Macy's Department Stores, and John Jacob Astor, perhaps the wealthiest man in the world. Just these three men have assets of over $500 million."

"Those men were on the ship, yes," the doctor said, "but this theory could have easily been conjured after the fact."

The Reverend shrugged. "Who knows? But according to this theory, it was believed that these three would use their wealth and influence to oppose a Federal Reserve Bank, as well as various wars that are being planned. It is believed that Captain Smith was also a Jesuit and was handpicked to steer this ship into disaster. His strong faith may have led him on this suicide mission."

Mr. Leblanc snorted and covered his derision by lifting his coffee cup to his mouth. "I doubt that any of this will ever be proven," he said.

"No," the Reverend admitted. "But it is interesting that apparently the *Titanic*'s flare guns fired white flares. Red is the emergency standard. Other colours were used for identification. White was to be used to signal "White Star Line." The *Californian* and other ships saw the white flares, but didn't consider them a distress call. All three men who were opposed to the Federal Reserve died during the sinking of the *Titanic*."

Mr. Wilkinson shifted forward. "That is fascinating, Reverend Holbrook. I also understand that when the ship was in trouble, more lives could have been saved if the radio operator on that nearby ship—the *Californian*—hadn't turned off his radio and gone to bed. Someone on that ship even reported to his captain—Captain Lord—that they saw the rockets going off, but they decided the ship was having a party. Perhaps the white flares were to blame for that. However, had they been paying more attention, they could have saved more of the passengers and crew before the ship sank."

"I don't imagine we will ever know all of the facts," Betsy said. "In a few years this will all be forgotten and no one will even think of it or talk about it again." That earned several thoughtful nods.

Henry Clarkson shifted the conversation with, "I wanted to bring my dog with me on this trip, but the cost was the same as the fare for a child. My parents couldn't afford the extra fare. The only people that can afford to bring their pets on these liners are the well off. It has made me wonder how many animals were on board the *Titanic* when she sank—has anyone heard? I'm sure people had their pets with them and I've wondered if any were saved. "

"I recall reading a report concerning the pets that perished that fatal night," Mr. Craig said. "I understand there were as many as nine dogs, about thirty cockerels, and a yellow canary. Apparently there was also a ship's cat named Jenny. One of the rescued crewmembers reported that three dogs and a canary were in the rescue boats when the *Carpathia* picked up the passengers. I guess, from that, that the cat did not survive. Too bad."

"Lucky for the canary, though," quipped the older Clarkson lad. Everyone laughed nervously. They were ready for a little relief from the sombre subject.

"Thank you for that information, Mr. Craig," said Henry. "I hope to be a veterinarian one day, and I am always looking out for how animals fare in these disastrous situations. They never do as well as humans."

The sun had set and most of the guests had drifted out of the dining hall. On that sobering note, those at Table 21 rose, bade each other good evening, and made their way out onto the deck.

CHAPTER ELEVEN: LOVERS AND OTHER STRANGERS

Many of the second class passengers on the *Olympic* were having a late-night brandy and listening to the final strains of music from the piano player in the library, taking a late night stroll on the deck, or preparing themselves for bedtime in their staterooms. Betsy fell into the latter category. As she slipped into her nightdress, she hoped that Rosa would have time to come for a visit after the evening chores were complete. She was anxious to hear Rosa's story about the *Titanic* rescue, but she knew those memories were very fresh and obviously very painful. *That must be what the sadness I have seen in Rosa is all about. I can't wait to hear what it was like.*

* * *

At the same moment Rosa, working in a neighbouring stateroom, was carrying a heavy burden around with her and longed to share it with someone who would not judge her. She dared not mention it to any of the staff—no one knew of her secret love affair. If they did, she knew she would be banned from the White Star Line forever. Could she tell her new friend Betsy? But how? *Can I tell Betsy about my dear, sweet Harold? Can I tell her everything about that horrible night? It would be such a relief, otherwise I may die from this guilt and loss I am burdened with.*

When the last of her passengers' requests had been fulfilled and the final bed turned down for the night, Rosa knocked on Betsy's door. "May I come in?" she queried through the door.

"Of course," Betsy called, as soon as she realized who it was.

Rosa stepped inside and smiled. *How should I broach the topic?* she wondered, nervous.

"I was hoping you'd stop by," Betsy said, crossing the cabin to take her hand and pull her over to the chair. She sat down on the edge of her bed.

The familiar gesture reassured Rosa. "How did you find your afternoon with the children today?" she asked.

Betsy's face lit up. "I enjoyed myself a great deal. The children were so outgoing and inquisitive. They really enjoyed my storytelling and I even got to show off my vast knowledge of quoits with the boys." She chuckled.

Rosa smiled. "I am glad. I'm sorry I went out and left you for a while. You see I started feeling panicky and had to go and see the ship's doctor. Betsy, I lost someone very wonderful the night the Titanic sank. I was rescued for some reason unknown to me. But he was last seen helping passengers get into the lifeboats. I keep wishing it was all a bad dream and that any minute I'll wake up."

"Oh I am so sorry for you Rosa. What was his name? Had you known him long?"

"His name was Harold and he was a junior third engineer, working down in the main engine room. She felt her cheeks turn red. "We had to be so careful onboard the ship," Rosa added. "Romance between crew members is strictly forbidden."

"How long did you know him and where did you meet?" Betsy asked inquisitively.

"We met on board one of the first ships I worked on, so I knew him for nearly three years. During our last voyage—the *Titanic*—things began to heat up for us. In fact he told me that when we reached New York he wanted to take me shopping for a ring. I can't believe he is gone. It just seems so unfair."

Betsy placed her hand on the young stewardess's arm. She sensed there was more that Rosa wanted to say but realized their relationship had already overstepped the established boundaries. "This must be so hard for you Rosa. I know what its like to lose a love. It will take some time for you to heal."

Rosa sighed. "How true that is. I adored Harold. I have had several other offers of marriage, one from a very wealthy first class passenger, but there really is no one else that held my interest as he did. "

Betsy nodded sympathetically. "I can appreciate what you must be experiencing. It can be so hard to get the right connection established with persons of the opposite sex. I really don't want to remain a spinster forever. A friend of mine is in Canada and she has written several times to say there are plenty of single men over there just waiting to meet a woman to marry."

"Oh, you are bound to find a really special man to marry you, Betsy. I just wish I could've heard those special words coming from my Harold's mouth. Why, when I stop and think about it, a captain, a purser, a chief steward, and at least half a dozen or more passengers have propositioned me in my time at sea. Not all marriage proposals!" Rosa smiled. "Too bad I wasn't more of a hussy! I could charge for my services and I might be a rich woman by now!" The two women laughed.

Rosa found she felt better, and Betsy looked tired. *No wonder,* Rosa thought gratefully, *after looking after all those children for me this afternoon!* "I'll leave you for the night," she said, rising. "Thank you for helping this afternoon. And...for listening."

"Oh, but you've listened to me, and have taken such good care of me," Betsy protested with a smile. "I am glad you chose to confide in me."

Rosa turned and a shadow passed over her face. "Good night, Betsy." *I wonder what she would think if I told her the whole story. I dare not. I haven't even the nerve to ask God's forgiveness.*

"Good night, Rosa."

CHAPTER TWELVE:
A QUIET DAY AT SEA

Betsy awoke the next morning and slowly stretched. *It's the last full day of the voyage,* she realized. *Tomorrow we arrive in New York.* She felt her heart beating faster as she sat up and swung her legs off the bed to stand—only to be overcome by waves of nausea. Surprise quickly gave way to alarm as she dashed to the basin in her room, barely making it before retching violently. *Good Lord,* she thought, *will I never get over this seasickness? I thought for sure I was cured by now. The ship isn't even swaying.*

Breakfast did not hold much appeal at this point. In fact, Betsy wondered if she could even make it down to the dining room, but she decided she'd better get dressed and give it a go. Her acquaintances at Table 21 would otherwise wonder what had become of her. *It was bad enough that I missed the first three days of this journey,* she thought with a touch of anger. *I am not going to spend my last day cooped up in my stateroom.* She dressed and braided and pinned her hair up in its usual style, all the while holding back the urge to be ill once more.

As she stepped into the hallway, she encountered her neighbours, Bernice Vaughn and her daughter Louisa. "Good morning," she said. "How are you both today?"

"We're just fine," replied Bernice.

"Oh Mama, that's her again. Our neighbour is the lady who told us the wonderful story in the gymnasium. You know, the one about the blue dress. I told you all about it!"

Bernice turned to Betsy. "You see what an impression you made on my daughter? She couldn't stop talking about the great story you told the kids in the gym the other day. She recounted the entire tale in detail over dinner that night and I must say, I too was impressed with your storytelling ability."

Betsy flushed, unused to such praise from anyone. "Oh, it was nothing; I just described a true event that occurred when I was a child. But I guess it planted some seeds of hope in the children's minds—that no matter how bad things may seem, there is always a chance that things will get better."

"Yes, that is such an important message. We hear too few of those messages these days, what with the world appearing to be gearing up for a terrible war and such. I was so relieved to be returning home to America at this time because of all the unrest."

"That was one reason my father wanted me to leave England," Betsy said as they all moved on to the dining saloon. "But to be honest, I'm not sure if I can say the same thing about Canada, which is where I am heading. Canada is part of the British Empire and they swear allegiance to King George, so I imagine it would be difficult for them to remain neutral in a war of that sort. I never mentioned my views about that to my father. I thought it best not to worry him unnecessarily."

Betsy said goodbye to the Vaughns and proceeded to Table 21 to see if any of the others had arrived. Although there was open seating, the *Titanic* passengers seemed to gravitate back to this table for most of their meals. Several people were already seated and she sat down next to Mrs. Wilkinson.

"How are you today?" asked Mrs. Wilkinson as Betsy pulled in her chair and placed her napkin on her lap.

"Strangely, I am feeling ill again after having recovered from seasickness yesterday—or so I thought," Betsy replied.

"Well, I have been told there are some things you can do to reduce the symptoms. You may have tried these already, but would you be interested in some free advice?" asked the older woman. Betsy nodded, willing to try anything at this point. She was disappointed that she'd felt ill for almost the entire voyage.

Mrs. Wilkinson leaned closer. "Well, for one thing, you should go on deck. It seems to the rocking of the ship causes more visual conflict indoors. And stay amidships or aft, where the total motion due to pitching and rolling is less severe. Oh, and don't sit or lie down indoors—lean against the cabin wall or roam passively, letting the motion toss you around. Anticipating the boat's motion is actually the natural cure for seasickness."

"I sure wish I had this advice a bit sooner" Betsy interjected.

"You can also try something called riding: Sit upright, and let your chest and neck muscles keep your upper body balanced over your hips as the boat moves. Once you get the rhythm, it's far less tiring than fighting to hang on. I know this can help, because I've experienced seasickness on almost every voyage I've been on. I do this and it really seems to help."

Doctor Stewart, seated across the table, had been listening. He added, "That's good advice, Mrs. Wilkinson. Betsy, I also suggest that you drink alcohol only in moderation. Alcohol has a direct effect on your inner ear, making you feel dizzy anytime you or the boat moves—especially if you overindulge."

Betsy smiled and thanked her tablemates for their advice. "I don't drink alcohol and I vow to spend as much of the day on deck, outdoors, as weather will permit. It appears to be a sunny but cool day, but I saw that there are plenty of warm blankets available on the deck chairs to snuggle up in."

The waiter appeared and she picked up the breakfast menu card on the table in front of her. There was a choice of fruit: baked apples, fresh fruit, and stewed prunes. "I'll have the prunes," she said, "but I think I will also pass on the oats and boiled hominy. What are the fish offerings?"

"We have herring, haddock, and smoked salmon. We also have some excellent meat dishes: ham, sausage, mutton, lamb, kidneys, and bacon," the waiter told her.

All of that struck her as too heavy for the way her stomach felt. "I believe I will have the omelette with cheese, and could you include a soda and sultana scone?"

Betsy picked at her food when it arrived but did manage to eat a little, finishing off with a cup of lemon-infused hot water that seemed to settle her stomach nicely; by the time breakfast was over, she told her fellow travellers she was starting to feel her old self.

Relieved to not only have a day all to herself but to feel well enough to enjoy it, she made her way to the library, where a serious-looking man with thick glasses was busying himself behind a small counter by the door. "I fancy a good read of a mystery story," Betsy replied when he asked her how he might help.

"We have quite a good selection, Miss. They are over there on that shelf." He pointed to a shelf on the far right of the room, which was small, but packed with what looked like many new books.

Delighted, Betsy browsed through the books and settled on a slightly worn copy of a Sherlock Holmes mystery by Scottish author and physician Sir Arthur Conan Doyle. She took it up to the desk.

The librarian looked up, and then moved over to check her book out for her. "Ah, good choice," he said.

"I've read a number of these Holmes mysteries," Betsy replied. "I really enjoy his astute logical reasoning and that he's a master at disguise."

"Holmes has had plenty of time to perfect his skills since his first appearance in 1887," the librarian quipped. "Doyle's creation has been in a total of four novels and fifty-six short stories."

Betsy hadn't been aware that Sir Arthur Conan Doyle had been so prolific. She made a mental note to track down more of the author's stories. "If I was ever to write a mystery story, I would hope it would be half as good as these," she said, holding up the book she was borrowing.

"Are you a writer?" asked the librarian. "I just spoke with a woman yesterday who is a mystery writer. Her name was Bernice something..." He paused in thought. "Ah—Vaughn, I believe."

"Oh yes, I've met her," Betsy said. "She occupies the cabin next to mine. At first I had no idea she was a writer. I'm not a writer myself. I have been employed as a governess for the past ten years and I am off to seek new employment in Canada."

"That's daring," the librarian observed with a smile. "What part of Canada are you going to?"

"I will be starting off in a place called Craven, Saskatchewan. I have a friend who is living in that area who has been encouraging me to come out. We'll see what happens after I get there. My only worry is the weather," Betsy confessed. "I hear it can be very cold there."

"Very daring," the librarian elaborated on his earlier opinion with a shiver and a smile. "Good luck to you."

"Thank you," Betsy said, and took her leave.

She spent much of the remainder of the day curled up in a blanket on the deck, lost in the world of *The Hound of the Baskervilles*.

CHAPTER THIRTEEN: SHIPS IN THE NIGHT

As evening fell, the sea was calm, the sky was clear, and after Rosa's work was complete for the night, she decided to stop by Betsy's cabin and invite her out to enjoy it with her.

"Betsy," she said when the woman she'd come to think of as a friend opened the door, "it's our last night at sea. Would you like to take a stroll with me on the promenade deck?"

"That would be wonderful. Just let me get a wrap."

Arm in arm they walked along the deck, stopping to look with wonder at the spray of stars splashed across the night sky."

"They go on forever, as far as the eye can see," Betsy said in a voice hushed with wonder.

"Isn't it a glorious sight?" Rosa agreed. "I am always amazed at the vastness of the night sky, out on the ocean." She pointed. "There's the Big Dipper over there. Do you see it?"

"Yes. And...there—the Seven Sisters, The Pleiades, but many people mistake it for The Little Dipper."

They both fell silent for a moment, soaking up the glory above them.

Finally Betsy turned to Rosa. "I could never have imagined how wondrous this would be. I've wondered what the sky was like the night the *Titanic* sank." She sighed. "I have thought about that horrid tragedy so often on this voyage. And you—to have been there..." She looked away, shaking her head. "I'm sorry. I've heard so much speculation about the sinking that I seem to have forgotten the pain it must bring you to talk about it."

Actually, Rosa wished she *could* talk about it, to someone. But to confide in a passenger... *Dare I break all the rules and tell the real truth?* she wondered. *What harm could there be? Betsy strikes me as someone who could handle hearing about the horrors of that night. Besides, we are like ships in the night. After tomorrow we will never cross paths again.* And so nervously, she began, knowing she was about to cross over a dangerous line.

"There is something that I would like to talk to you about. I haven't been able to speak to anyone about the last night on the *Titanic*, but it is troubling me greatly. Could I confide in you and bend your ear one more time?" Rosa asked.

Betsy's eyebrows went up, her interest aroused. She nodded and said, "Oh, do go on."

Rosa drew a deep, trembling breath and gripped the railing, staring out into the star-limned sea. "I have actually been quite petrified on this voyage," she admitted. "I haven't been able to sleep, I have no appetite, and flashes of horror keep cropping up in my mind regarding the events of that horrible night. I was one of the few crew members rescued from the sinking."

Betsy reached out and rested a hand on her arm.

"It was horrifying." Her voiced cracked but she continued. "The White Star Line managers thought I should be placed on this ship right away or, they feared, I might never set sail again. They were probably right! But I am not really sure I should even be sailing on this voyage."

"I can't believe how brave you were to set sail again so soon," Betsy said as Rosa stopped to collect herself. She wore an expression of compassion and sympathy.

Rosa drew a tremulous breath. She hadn't thought it would be this hard, that it would rekindle such vivid impressions from that night. "I have so many memories of that horrid night and all that ensued. I just can't get them out of my mind. I thought maybe if I told my story to someone, it would help me to make some sense of it." She turned to face Betsy. "There is no one else I am close enough to whom I can discuss this with just now. The doctor is nice but he just gave me a sedative to help me sleep. Are you sure you don't mind if I go over the events of the sinking and my rescue? You are like a sister to me. Even if its just for the duration of this passage."

"Oh, please do go on," Betsy said gently. "Right from the moment I first met you I sensed you were sad somehow, melancholy. The maiden voyage of the *Titanic* was a much-celebrated event that ended in such suffering and loss. How awful that you had to endure that experience. Tell me whatever you need to; your words are safe with me."

Rosa smiled fleetingly. "Thank you. It *was* such an exciting launch! When the ship first set sail from Southampton on April 10, we had on board an amazing group of gentry, many of whom were travelling back to America after wintering in Europe. But there was what might have been a portent of things to come, as well—when the ship left Berth 44, we passed very close to two ships that were moored alongside each other in Berth 38—the *Oceanic* and the *New York*. The water was so churned up by the *Titanic*'s powerful propellers that the other ships broke free of their moorings and were drawn toward *Titanic*. I remember hearing a loud snap, then seeing the *New York* swing out toward the *Titanic*. We all thought there was going to be a collision for sure."

"How did *Titanic* manage to avoid that?" inquired Betsy, intrigued.

Rosa smiled with a proud memory. "Captain Smith responded immediately. He ordered that the propellers be shut down. A tugboat—the *Vulcan*—that was assisting with the departure turned around and got a wire rope on the port quarter of the *New York*. That rope broke, but the tugboat men were on top of things; they got a second wire onto the ship and stopped her from drifting. When she was stopped she was but four feet away from the *Titanic*. I remember thinking that it was not a good omen to have such a close call only minutes after leaving the dock."

" I sometimes wish that I could sense things about to happen," Betsy remarked, "but to be perfectly honest, when I was told I could not sail on the *Titanic*'s maiden voyage, the only emotions I experienced were disappointment and anger. I didn't sense any danger at all. Were you aware of anyone who had any premonitions or bad feelings?"

"Yes, there seemed to be more of these than usual. But then again, after a disaster like this, anyone who had bad feelings about the voyage will be more acutely aware of them after the fact. When nothing bad happens, people may be more likely to forget they ever had such feelings."

"True," Betsy said.

Rosa continued. "I do know that after the rescue, on board the ship that rescued us—the *Carpathia*—a number of the *Titanic* passengers and crew shared stories of having had premonitions or bad feelings prior to the sailing. Art Lewis, one of the stewards, said that prior to the voyage, he asked his wife to put his white star on his uniform cap and while she was doing that, it fell to pieces. He said his wife exclaimed, 'I don't like this.'"

"Another crew member said that he always thought it was bad luck to have his wife see him off to sea and forbade her from ever doing so. On the day that *Titanic* sailed, she had insisted on coming down to the pier for some strange reason. He said he felt sick when he saw her there and was sure something would go wrong."

"Yes, no doubt," Betsy said. "Do go on with your story, Rosa."

Realizing she'd digressed to avoid reliving her nightmare, Rosa nodded. "Alright. Where was I? Oh yes, we had just set sail. The next couple of days of the voyage progressed extremely well. In fact, all of the stewards and stewardesses were convinced that when the gratuities were handed out at the end of the journey, we would come out much ahead of any trip any of us had made to date. Our wages are so low, we rely heavily on tips to make a decent living. That's one aspect of this position I really hate."

"Were most of these employees women?" inquired Betsy. "In general, women's wages are so much less than men's, sometimes even for doing the exact same work."

"No," replied Rosa. "In fact, of the 898 crew members on board the *Titanic*, only twenty-three were women. Eighteen of these were steward-esses, and there was one first class matron, a masseuse who was an attendant in the Turkish baths, and two women who worked as cashiers in the Ritz Restaurant."

"Were all of the women crew rescued after the sinking?" asked Betsy.

"No, three of the female crew did not survive. One woman was a close friend of mine, working as a stewardess down in steerage. I learned that she stayed below deck with an ailing passenger, even when ordered to go above. That would have been her nature. She was one of the most dedicated people I have ever known." That memory broke her control. Rosa began to sob, and tears that had been pent up ever since that fateful night flowed.

Betsy placed a comforting arm around her shoulders, and handed her a hanky that had been tucked in her bosom. Rosa took it gratefully.

When she'd regained her composure, Rosa continued. "I had finished my duties for the night and... well I" Rosa caught her breath. "I eventually went down into the 'glory hole,' the name we use for staff quarters. I talked with my roommate about how much better these quarters were than on any ship I had been on and she agreed." Rosa paused. There was a part of the story she had to leave out. Even Betsy wouldn't understand. "A short while later I climbed into my upper bunk. It was just before midnight. That was when we felt the sudden jarring of the ship."

"Was it a significant jolt?" asked Betsy, her eyes wide with fascination.

"No it wasn't really that hard at all. In fact it felt like a light brushing had occurred along one side of the hull." Rosa settled into an account similar to what she'd reported to officials after the sinking; the more objective litany felt more comfortable to her right now. "The ship's engines were immediately turned off and Norma and I exchanged looks. A bedroom steward named Stanley knocked on our door and advised us that we would be needed, as the ship may be in serious trouble. We quickly got dressed and went to rouse our assigned passengers. As we were told to do, we explained they were to get dressed warmly, leave all personal belongings behind, and come up to Deck 6 for further directions. Everyone was groggy from interrupted sleep; the children were especially bewildered. But amazingly, nobody panicked. We got everyone into life jackets, but people were calm and even joking. I think nobody realized the danger of the situation yet."

"It had been touted as unsinkable, after all," Betsy said.

"Really, none of us could believe what was happening. It felt surreal. The band had been playing in the first class dining room and someone had ordered them to reconvene on the deck, so for the next two hours, while people were loaded into lifeboats, we heard their music being played—minus the piano player, of course, as there was no piano on deck.

"All the while we were directed to tell people that the life vests and the lifeboats were a precautionary measure only. We also told them that there were a number of boats in the vicinity and if necessary, they would come to our aid immediately. We really believed that, in fact. Only later did we learn that wasn't true. I guess it helped keep the passengers calm—some even joked around as they made their way to the upper deck."

Rosa paused and moistened her lips. The horror was coming closer now... "As it became clearer that only women and children were going to make it into the lifeboats, I noticed that wives started to cling to their spouses, reluctant to leave them behind on deck. The men were all very supportive, though, and encouraged the women to get into the boats as we requested." The next memory made her lip curl in disapproval. "One man came rushing out dressed as a woman and jumped into one of the boats."

"Oh my!" Betsy exclaimed. "That was nervy, to set aside one's pride so."

Rosa nodded, appreciating the new spin Betsy's perspective put on the man's behaviour. *He was as frightened as the rest of us, but weaker. Will he live comfortably with himself, wherever he is now?* she wondered. "No one was pleased," she said aloud, "but they couldn't do anything about it by then. They just let him go."

"There had been multiple practice drills before the ship sailed to educate us all about how to handle such a disaster but honestly, no one ever dreamed we would be called into action on that ship. So I know there were many mistakes made."

"Like what, for example?" asked Betsy.

"For one thing, there weren't enough lifeboats to accommodate the number of passengers and crew. We knew that ahead of time. There were twenty boats—sixteen regular ones and four inflatables— and if each took on the maximum of sixty people, that would only have accommodated twelve hundred in total. The *Titanic* had over 2,350 people altogether. Then, when the boats were being filled with people, most of them were lowered with only thirty or forty people in them. Boat Number One had only twelve people in it and of those, seven of them were crew members. Had the boats been filled to capacity, there would have been many more lives saved."

"That's terrible," Betsy murmured, her eyes going distant for a moment as she did the math. "Which lifeboat were you in?"

"I was assigned to Lifeboat Number 16. My room-mate was assigned to the same boat. I wanted to do a final check on the passengers in my section so, so I was later getting into the boat. Norma was already there. Just as the boat was about to be lowered into the water, someone rushed over and placed a small baby in Norma's arms. Of course she held onto the wee thing for dear life, but we kept wondering what had become of its mother. We knew she would be desperately looking for her little one."

Betsy's brows drew together at that and she looked thoughtful, and Rosa remembered her fondness for children, and that she dearly wanted to start a family of her own. "Did you ever learn of their fate—the babe's or the mother's—afterward?"

Rosa nodded. "After a fashion. I'll get to it."

Betsy nodded, once, then urged, "Do go on."

"Once the boat was in the ocean we began to row quite quickly to get away from the ship. In the distance we could see another ship that appeared to be standing still. We were sure that they had seen the flares that were lit on our ship and they would be coming to our rescue any minute. We found out later that that was the *Californian*, a ship that had sent many warning alerts to the *Titanic* several hours before. The radio operator had, however, turned off their radio and gone to sleep, so he didn't hear our distress calls. They saw our distress flares, but apparently they thought we were having a party on board. It wasn't uncommon to light flares during a party."

"Some party you were having!" quipped Betsy.

"Someone else even said they saw a second ship in the area. They referred to it as a ghost ship because nothing else was known about it. The truth about that will likely never be revealed. The facts surrounding the *Californian* will no doubt be a part of the inquiry being held in New York concerning the whole affair."

"And when *Titanic* sank?" Betsy asked softly.

"That is the worst memory I have of that night. We were not in the lifeboat for very long when I noticed that instead of five rows of lights on the ship, there were only four. That was when it began to really hit me. That and the sights and sounds of people starting to jump overboard will haunt me forever. Many of those who jumped survived in the water for a short spell and we could hear them calling out for help. The women in my boat were all sobbing. Some of those calls could have been from their husbands and fathers."

"I wanted my father to come with me," Betsy said, barely above a whisper. Her eyes were still distant, perhaps envisioning possibilities.

For Rosa, they'd been reality. "One man actually made it to our boat swimming, and as we pulled him in, all of the women anxiously looked to see if he was someone they knew. But it turned out he was a crew member. He was a friend of Harold's—that engineer that I...well, that I had become close to—and I asked him if he knew whether Harold had made it into one of the lifeboats. He said he thought he had been assigned to one over on the port side, but he wasn't sure. Just hearing that gave me some hope. For a while. It was only later that I found out he gave up his seat in the boat so that another women or child could be saved."

Tears gently streamed down Rosa's face. Betsy handed her a handkerchief she pulled from her sleeve.

"I spent the rest of the night shaking in fear and with cold as we sat in the dark in that lifeboat. After about eight hours the *Carpathia* picked us up. Norma was still clutching the baby against the lifebelt she was wearing as she was helped aboard. A woman leapt at her and grabbed the baby, then rushed off with it. It turns out that she put the baby down on the deck of the *Titanic* while she went off to fetch something, and when she came back the wee thing was gone. We were pretty frozen and numb and it didn't occur to us at the time that the mother never even thanked us for saving her baby."

Rosa again began to sob quietly. Betsy gathered her into her arms and held her tightly, and Rosa allowed the tears to flow unabashedly. The moon had disappeared behind a fresh crop of evening clouds. The seas remained calm. Several minutes passed before Rosa pulled back, nodded in silent gratitude, then looked at Betsy. She was trembling.

"There is something more, Betsy. Something I swore never to tell a living soul. I don't know why, but I need to get this off my chest. I..." She stopped.

"Go on," urged Betsy. "It will do you good to get it out."

"Well, there is a piece of the story I have not told you. You see, in my heart, I believe that I was likely responsible for the *Titanic*'s sinking."

Betsy took her gently by the shoulders. "Oh Rosa, you couldn't possibly be. Why would you say such a thing?"

"Well, shortly before ten p.m. that night, I received a message from my Harold that he would like me to come down to the engine room for a visit. It had been a very calm sea and we were nearing the end of our voyage. I was so excited that he wanted to see me—I actually wondered if it signalled a change in our up and down relationship. Besides, I had never seen where he works. I finished my chores, changed out of my uniform, and went to the area above the engine room.

"I climbed down the stairs the way Harold had instructed me to and he was waiting at the bottom. Because it was so quiet, the other two engineers in the room had been told they could leave their shift early, so we were alone. Harold took my hand and showed me the various engine controls. It was so amazing."

"That makes me realize I haven't even thought about how this ship runs," Betsy commented. "Everything is so comfortable and pleasant up here that the nuts and bolts of how it's made possible escape my mind." She shook her head quickly. "I'm sorry to have interrupted. Continue, Rosa."

Rosa nodded, and felt her cheeks heat. "Well, suddenly, we were both overcome with emotion. Harold took me in his arms right there and kissed me tenderly. He reached over and set the ship controls to stay the course automatically." A surge of panic made her pause. *I've gone too far,* she thought.

Betsy was staring at her, her expression a mixture of shock and puzzlement. "Rosa, you need to get this off your chest. I promise you it will never leave my lips, if you are worried about that."

"Oh Betsy, thank you. I just hope you won't think ill of me once you know the sordid truth."

"Rosa, I'm the last person on earth that should judge your behaviour. Especially concerning your relationships with the opposite sex."

Rosa felt weak with relief. She slowly exhaled, then said, "Well, there was a small closet off to one side, and he took me by the hand and led me there. On the floor was a sleeping bag, rolled out. It was used by the engineers to take short naps when things were quiet in the engine room. There was only a small bit of light shining through the glass of the door."

She stopped, clearing her throat to conceal her hesitation. "It all happened so fast that I didn't have time to think about what we were doing. We held each other tightly, at which point I strongly suggested we should stop. Harold seemed not to hear me. Soon we were both completely swept away with emotion. I doubt if we were in there for more than about ten minutes. We made passionate love and for those few minutes, I imagined that we really were a couple and that he really did love me. Harold never openly expressed his love for me. But I knew deep down he cared. I just can't believe still that he died before we had a chance to be together properly. The only thing I have to remember him by is this." Rosa plucked a chain out from beneath her uniform. Attached to the fine silver stand was a small silver heart-shaped locket. She opened it and Betsy saw a small picture of a red-headed young man. "Harold?" she asked. Rosa nodded.

"But why would that make you think that you were at fault for the sinking, Rosa?"

"After the rescue, the second radio operator and I were seated next to each other on the deck of the *Carpathia*. In reliving the events of the evening, he shared with me that at about ten p.m. that night, the time Harold and I were engaged - he was notified by another ship that there was severe ice ahead. He immediately passed the information on to Captain Smith. He said he was there when Captain Smith issued the orders down to the engine room to cut the engines and slow the boat down. He said that the boat continued on the same speed and in his view, that is what contributed to the terrible damage the ship sustained at the time of the collision. He said he was puzzled, that the orders seemed not to have been followed, and wondered why."

"Oh my word!" exclaimed Betsy. "Are you suggesting that because he was making love to you, Harold missed hearing the order and so never cut the engines back? Is that what you are trying to tell me?"

"Yes," sobbed Rosa. "A foolish, reckless mistake that may have cost hundreds of lives."

Betsy felt weak at the knees. *If all of this is true, Rosa could indeed have played a significant role in causing the Titanic to meet her fatal end,* she thought. The magnitude of Rosa's confession became clear and for perhaps the only time in her life, Betsy had no words.

CHAPTER FOURTEEN:
THE VOYAGE ENDS

Even before she was fully awake, Betsy remembered why this was one of the most exciting days of her life. *This is the end. Our ship will finish the voyage. After I clear Customs and Immigration I will board the train for Canada. I can't believe the journey is nearing its end,* she thought.

She looked out the cabin window, hoping to see New York's harbour as the ship sailed into it, and was disappointed that it was foggy. Betsy looked closely for the famous Statue of Liberty and New York's skyline, but she couldn't identify them in the mist. She turned from the window and finished packing the rest of her belongings, then waited for the word that it was time to disembark.

The expected knock came. When she opened the door, a steward waiting there announced instead, "There is going to be a delay while the immigration and health records are checked."

"Very well. Thank you." Betsy shut the door and crossed to sit on her bed. She wondered if the coming check would make the passage through Customs go faster, once they'd docked, or if there would be another delay there, as well. Another wave of nausea suddenly overcame her. *I can't believe I am still feeling ill,* she thought. *I hope I don't look sick; what a time to feel ill!*

As she stood to check her appearance in the mirror, Betsy was shocked when the button on her skirt popped off and rolled across the floor. She bent over to pick it up. "Good Lord. I don't have time to sew this back on," she muttered. Instead she opened her case and hurriedly pulled out another skirt and donned it. She was closing her suitcase once again when the second knock came.

Betsy soon found herself moving toward the disembarkation area of the ship. She focused her gaze on the row of ship employees standing in line by the door until she found Rosa, and then made a beeline to her new friend. The two women embraced and Betsy slipped a one-pound note into her hand as a gratuity. "Thank you so much for all of your kindness," she said. "You made this entire trip bearable. I shall miss you." Wiping away tears, they both vowed to stay in touch via correspondence.

As she stepped off the ramp, Betsy was directed to join the other Canada-bound passengers in a special holding area. She was delighted to be joined in the line by Pierre Leblanc, the young man heading for Montreal. Pierre offered to carry her suitcase for her and she gratefully accepted. Her shipboard illness seemed to have drained much of her strength; even the exertion of disembarking left her knees feeling wobbly—she felt like a new colt trying to stand for the first time. *Perhaps now I have to get my land legs,* she mused.

She was grateful that she and Pierre were processed through the terminal at Ellis Island quickly, thanks to their documents having already been checked over before leaving the ship— Betsy had heard rumours of people being detained for hours upon arrival. Betsy and Pierre were directed to waiting carts and taken directly to the train station, where their Canada-bound train arrived after about an hour.

The pair boarded the same coach. It was heading first for Montreal, where she and Pierre would part ways and Betsy would carry on across Canada to the Prairies. "Let's sit together in one of these double seats so that we will face each other. That way we'll both have a window seat to get a good view. I've read we'll be passing through the upper New York state countryside, over the St. Lawrence River, and into lower Quebec" said Pierre.

Though frequently punctuated with expressions of awe at what passed by their window, Pierre and Betsy passed much of the trip in comfortable conversation. Both confessed to excitement and trepidation about what they might encounter at their respective destinations.

"I received some training as a Hudson Bay representative before leaving England," Pierre said, "but I have no idea what nature of people I will be dealing with. Most of them will be native Indians."

Betsy smiled. "You know that the portrayal of them as wild savages has been proven false, right?"

"Yes, they told us that many of them are in fact quite civilized by now," Pierre replied. "Many have been converted to Catholicism and are adopting the white man's healthier ways of eating. Most have been given their own land on reservations now, so the need for territorial wars is over."

This fascinated Betsy. "I haven't thought about encountering Indians in Saskatchewan. Are there many of these people on the Prairies?" she asked.

Pierre shrugged. "I'm not sure. I do know there are different tribes in different regions of North America."

Betsy made a promise to herself to learn more about these people and their strange customs.

When they arrived in Montreal, Pierre and Betsy said their farewells to one another and then Betsy departed on a westbound train an hour later. It had been pleasant having a familiar travel companion for part of the journey, but now she was on her own and looking forward to getting some much-needed sleep. At twenty-eight, she was still young enough to curl her legs beneath her. She loosened her belt and before long, the rhythmic clack-clack the train made going over the tracks lulled her into a fitful sleep.

CHAPTER FIFTEEN:
THE BROWNS OF
SASKATCHEWAN

May 24, 1912

Fifty-one-year-old Mary Ann Brown woke to the sound of roosters crowing in the yard and out of habit, glanced at the photo of her and her late husband that sat on her bedside table. She sighed and lay there for a few minutes longer, reflecting on the previous few years. *I don't know how I survived losing my Sammy,* she thought. *If only he hadn't gone out in that storm.*

Four years ago, her husband had taken the horse and buggy into Lumsden to buy medicine for one of the boys who was ill. Before he could get home, the storm hit and he was drenched in the downpour and pounded with hail the size of marbles. Pneumonia set in and he became very ill, and a week later he died in his sleep. He was only fifty-one.

"Oh, how I miss you," Mary Ann murmured, lifting the photo to study his face.

The people of Craven were in awe of this strong, hard-working woman. They were particularly impressed with her strong family values. "I am amazed with how she and her five sons have formed that seeding outfit. They have planted most of the crops in the whole region here," remarked one of her neighbours.

Widow Brown and her 7 offspring.

It had all been working out fairly well. They had managed without any extra help. Until now. The work of keeping up the housework, feeding all the family, handling the scheduling of the work for neighbouring farmers, and just running a farm—it was getting to be too much for her. Finally deciding that she needed extra help, Mrs. Brown had registered an ad with the agency that offered employment to people in the United Kingdom.

She rose, washed and dressed and tied up her hair, then went out to the kitchen to start breakfast for her only daughter Vera and the five boys. Vera joined her moments later and after a quick smile, started doing her share of the preparations.

"George, please get the buggy ready to pick up the new hired hand," Mary Ann asked her second oldest, George, when he walked in with a canvas sling full of kindling. She eyed him up and down. He had on a freshly laundered shirt and fresh pants. She didn't say anything, not wanting to embarrass him. He was shy, especially around women, but Mary Ann trusted that he could handle the task of picking up the new British immigrant she had hired to help on the farm.

He did not seem that interested in girls and indeed, she hoped he would put off meeting a girl and getting married for a long time to come. She had come to rely on him so much on the farm. Her oldest boy, Allen, was much less reliable and in fact seemed to suffer from some mild form of unexplained muscle weakness.

"And after you collect her, please come straight back home. It will nearly be dinnertime and she will be exhausted after her long journey from England."

Vera looked up quickly. "Oh Mother, may I go with him? Miss Oakes would likely welcome another woman for company, and someone has to keep an eye on our George, here, who's *much* too handsome for his own good." She reached out to ruffle her older brother's hair, but he ducked back with a grin. George was indeed handsome. He had a broad forehead, wide eyes, and lips that were full and distinct. He was three years older than Vera, so Vera heard all about what husband material her brother was from her girlfriends.

"I'll need you here today, Vera," Mary Ann said, not looking up from the eggs she was monitoring in the fry pan. "Besides, there won't be enough room in the buggy for another passenger besides Miss Oakes and her trunk."

Vera didn't try to hide her disappointment, but she didn't protest, either. Instead she stuck her tongue out at George, who returned the gesture as he swaggered out of the kitchen. He loved Vera to pieces, but a day alone was a rare and precious treat.

George strolled out to the barn, where his brother Norman was doing chores. "I'm on my way into town now. Sure am happy to get away for the day," he said smugly.

Norman gaped at him a moment. "Take me along," he finally said.

George shook his head. "There's a few shops I want to stop at and it's rare that I get to do that without Mother or any of you kids along."

"I'm not a kid," Norman protested. "I'm sixteen. Let me come."

Again George shook his head. "No room for you. Vera pleaded to go with me too, but Mother pointed out that there wouldn't be enough room for Miss Betsy and her trunk with an extra passenger in the buggy."

Norman had no argument for that. He hung his head and returned to pitching hay.

George lifted the bridle from a peg by the entrance to Nellie's stall and stepped inside. "Whoa, Nellie," he soothed as caught the gentle mare's bobbing head and slipped the bridle on. He led her out to the two-seater buggy, backed her between the shafts, and harnessed her up.

The sun was shining and George smiled. *That's a good omen,* he thought. There was, however, a brisk prairie breeze blowing, so he tossed a couple of throws into the buggy in case the new hired hand felt chilled. Then he climbed into the buggy and he and the mare trotted off down the lane.

Twenty minutes later, George made his first stop, a social visit at the blacksmith's, where his best friend William Seed was apprenticing. The two young men heartily shook hands and George explained the nature of his mission into town that day. William expressed envy at George's freedom to have even part of a day to himself.

"I'm working eight to ten hours a day, six days a week, and I'm still not making enough money to adequately support Velma," William said, referring to his bride of a few months.

"But when you've finished the apprenticeship, you'll know enough to set up your own smithy," George reminded him. "You'll probably still be working long hours, but it will all go into your pocket."

"True, that," William said. "But until then—" he cast a glance over his shoulder "—I'm at old Farley's mercy."

"I won't keep you, then," George said, not wanting to hold him up from his work.

"Come by the house this Saturday evening," William said as George climbed back into the buggy. "We'll catch up, play a game of caroms."

"I'll do that," George said. "I've just completed making a new caroms board, and I need to test it out in competition.[1]" With a wave, George was off and heading for his next stop.

He had a bit of a sweet tooth and whenever he had the chance, he liked to stop at the soda shop, where jars of hard candy lined the countertop. Liquorice was his favourite. After tying up the horse, he went inside and waited in a line to be served. The young

---

1   The square board with pockets in the corners was believed to have been derived from the game of billiards.

woman behind the counter looked familiar and he suddenly realized she was Martha, the daughter of the pastor at his church. She had moved into town the past year to look for work.

"Hello Martha," he said when it was his turn to be served.

She beamed at him. "Why, hello George. What brings you all the way down here?"

"I've come to meet the 3:45 train from out east. My mother has hired a new farmhand and she's arriving all the way from England today. I thought I would pick up some sweets to offer her when she gets here. I'll take some home to Vera, as well."

"Great; what flavours would you like?" asked Martha, sweeping her hand above the row of candy jars.

George picked out four different kinds of candy and bought a small bag of each. "And a can of chewing tobacco," he added, pointing to his pre-ferred brand. His mother was dead set against him smoking, but she couldn't say too much about him keeping a wad of chew in his cheek, especially if he hid it well.

"Well, I must be off," declared George after they'd exchanged a few pleasantries. "Will I see you in church on Sunday?"

Martha shook her head. "No, I'm going to the Pentecostal church in Regina now. In fact, I'm planning on marrying my fiancé there later in the summer. My father would have preferred to marry us in his church, but I want him there simply as my dad, to give me away."

George nodded, thanked her for the candy, and said goodbye and good luck with the wedding.

As he climbed into the buggy he thought, *I'm eighteen and already many of my peers are settling down and having families. I haven't even had a serious girlfriend. Maybe I should start looking around soon.*

A leather cobbler in the centre of the town was his next destination. His shoes had become so worn that the toes of one foot were exposed to the elements and the soles were worn thin. The purchase of new boots was considered to be the ultimate luxury and he had pleaded long and hard with his mother to convince her that this was a worthwhile family expense. He had funds of his own saved from his labours, but he was reluctant to start spending any of this money. It was earmarked to eventually fund the down payment on a piece of land to call his own. That was his dream. Until then, he was content to work with his mother and brothers on the family farm.

The shop owners were courteous and friendly. They brought out many different types of boots to try on, only to find that George's size 13 feet would only fit into a very few styles. But he found one pair he liked and after determining that they fit, George decided to buy them. He kept them on and put his old boots into a trash bin that he spotted on the premises. He was not sure why, but it seemed important to have on new boots, this particular day.

George thanked the shop owners and climbed back into his parked buggy. Just as he was pulling out from the side of the road, a small black puppy darted out onto the road beside the buggy, and when he heard the puppy scream he realized one of the back wheels had run over the poor creature. He reined in Nellie, hopped down, and went back to find the puppy. It was lying on the road just behind his right rear wheel, whining piteously. "Poor thing," he murmured, bending down to pick up the small ball of fur. He cradled it in his arms and the pup stirred and turned its head and licked his hand. "Oh, you are a cute little thing," he crooned. "I wonder who you belong to. I have half a mind to take you back to the farm with me, where you will be safe."

A shopkeeper came out to the road at this point and claimed to be the puppy's owner, along with the other five pups from that litter. "If you want him, he's yours," he declared. "I'm trying to get rid of them 'cause they've just been weaned."

George was thrilled. "I do want him," he said of the pup that had begun squirming in his arms, trying to lick his face. "I think he ran under my wheel, but he seems okay." After checking the pup over and realizing his injuries were superficial, George made a bed for him in the back of the buggy. "We'll figure out a name for you later, little one," he said softly, stroking the trembling pup. George and his new friend left the area at a slow trot.

The 3:45 train from the east would be arriving at the station soon - time to get to the train station. He had only a vague description of this woman he was to pick up and he did not want to be late.

He arrived at the station with plenty of time to spare. "You'll be safest if you come with me," he said to the puppy as he lifted it out of its nest on the throws. Carrying the pup in his arms, he entered the station and found a place to sit. A baggage handler sat down next to him, also awaiting the arrival of the 3:45. After nodding a hello, George let his eyes wander around the station.

The railroad had been completed in 1883, just twenty-nine years ago. And the province only joined Canada in 1905, just seven years ago. George recalled his parents saying that when they moved here from Ontario in 1892, Regina had only just recently acquired its regal name. Until 1882 it was called "Pile o' Bones," in reference to the large pile of buffalo and bison bones that had been stacked there over the years. Now it was a town of over four thousand people and served as the capital of the province of Saskatchewan.

A whistle moaned in the distance and George felt his pulse quicken. *Why am I so nervous?* he wondered. He wiped his sweaty hands on his pants and, picking up the pup, he walked out to the platform. The train was pulling in. Steam poured from the engine and the wheels came to a slow, screeching halt.

George scanned the faces of the disembarking passengers. Some were obviously from far distant lands and he heard bits and pieces of languages that sounded like German, Dutch, French, Swedish and Polish. Word had obviously gotten out about the cheap land and employment opportunities in the Prairies.

Soon he spotted what had to be her. She was very small but carried her head high in an almost regal fashion. She was wrapped in a long dark coat with a lovely feathered hat and matching gloves. She was not what he was expecting at all, although he would be hard pressed to say just what he actually did expect. It was just that she was coming to work as a hired hand and by Jove, he thought she looked more like a fine English lady than a common labourer.

George approached her. "Betsy Oakes?" he asked.

"Why, yes," she replied with a lovely, lilting English accent. "Have you been sent by the Browns to collect me and my things?"

"Yes. I'm George Brown, Mary Ann's second oldest. Here. Why don't you carry this puppy and I will carry that bag for you. It looks heavy."

"What a cute puppy!" exclaimed Betsy. "What's his name?"

"He doesn't have one yet. I just acquired him today. Hey, maybe you might be interested in naming him."

Betsy smiled. "I love small animals," she said, gazing down at the puppy squirming in her arms. "We could wind up being best friends, you and I." She glanced shyly up at George. He was tall, probably six feet, making it difficult to look directly into his eyes, but she could see that they were deep blue and pensive. She noticed his pressed shirt and shiny new boots.

They both looked to see where the baggage was being off-loaded and together went to find her trunk. Once the bags, trunk, Betsy, and the wee dog were safely ensconced in the buggy, George announced they were off on the eight-mile trek out to Craven.

On the way he answered her many questions about the farm and its occupants. He told her about the death of his father and brother. "My mother has a stern exterior, but underneath, she's actually very soft and understanding," he said. He described with pride the services the family fulfilled in the whole of the farming district. He even disclosed to her his desire to own his own plot of land one day soon. Betsy was impressed. He seemed so young and yet for his age, so mature.

She was tired and nodded off to sleep for the final half-hour of her arduous journey—it had been over a week since she left home. It all seemed so far away now.

She awoke just as George was turning onto the final road leading to the farm. "You must be very tired from your long journey," he observed when he saw she was awake. "We're almost there, Miss Betsy."

They had left Regina and its outskirts behind. Now Betsy gazed out with wonder at the flat expanse of prairie that extended around her in every direction. With no hills or trees to block the view, she found being on the open prairie was like being on the ocean, only instead of waves, one saw only fields of newly planted hay waving in the breeze.

As they turned down the winding lane leading to the Brown farm, Betsy could see a row of farm machinery that stretched nearly a city block long. She had no idea what the various pieces of equipment were used for, but just their size and sheer number impressed her.

The farmhouse and barn loomed ahead. The house was a white, two-storey wood frame structure with black trim and shutters. The front porch had an open deck where two rocking chairs were perched. Chequered curtains covered the downstairs windows. The house appeared huge to Betsy, in contrast to the small stone cottages and row houses of England.

The barn sat several hundred feet from the house. As they pulled into the yard, Betsy could see that there were cows and horses in the adjacent yard and a pen full of hogs next to the barn. Chickens ran and squawked everywhere.

As George helped her off the cart, the entire Brown clan came out to greet her. George introduced each sibling who stepped forward and shook her hand.

"This," George said, playfully ruffling the hair of a lanky boy who hurried forward first, hand outstretched, a serious expression on his smooth face, "is Stanley, the baby of the family."

Grimacing, Stanley dodged George's hand. "I'm no baby! I'm thirteen," he said to Betsy as she shook his hand.

"I'm pleased to meet you, young man," Betsy said, and Stanley beamed.

"And Harry," George said as a young man who looked to be close to George in age came forward and exchanged a familiar look with his brother, which confirmed their birth order for Betsy; these two boys had grown up together.

Harry nodded to Betsy as he gave her hand one firm shake. "Pleased to meet you, Miss Oakes."

"Please, call me Betsy," she said.

Harry smiled and shyly replied, "Betsy." He turned as yet another boy came forward. "This is Norman."

"He's sixteen," George supplied, "and thinks he knows all about the world."

Norman turned slowly from his brothers to Betsy and said with a smirk, "Truth is, I do."

Betsy chuckled. "Pleased to meet you, worldly Norman."

She was a little relieved when a young woman came forward to meet her. *So many males in this household!* she thought.

"Don't mind Norman," she said. "He's barely older than Stanley, so he likes to put on airs." Norman sputtered, but the girl turned blithely back to Betsy, shutting him out. "I'm Vera."

"Very pleased to meet you, Vera," Betsy said, with feeling.

A man closer to Betsy's age came forward last; he was thin and stooped and he walked as though he had elastic bands for leg muscles. "Allen," he said, a slightly shaky hand extended.

"Pleased, to meet you, Allen."

The back door opened and an older woman stepped onto the porch, wiping her hands on her apron. "Miss Betsy Oakes," she said as she came forward, her face all serious and business like. "I'm Mary Anne Brown. Come inside and I'll show you around. George, boys, bring in her bags and trunk for her and put them in her room." As she turned, Betsy couldn't help but notice her plain dyed brown collarless cotton dress and well-worn leather shoes. Her jewellery - a plain gold wedding band. *So different from the way English women dress,* she thought.

* * *

Surprisingly, it didn't take long for Betsy to adapt to her new life on the prairie farm. She thought it was ironic that her new employment bore one similarity to the position she had in England: just one daughter. All similarities ended there, however. Living with so many boys was different. The work was vastly different. Although Mrs. Brown had originally advertised for domestic help, Betsy seemed to take to the farm chores more readily. She found she loved collecting fresh eggs in the barnyard every day, milking the cows, tending to the pigs, and collecting water out of the well.

That suited the Browns just fine, as it freed the boys to work in the fields and keep up with maintenance of the machinery. Betsy did help in the kitchen at mealtime. She loved the hustle and bustle there. The kitchen was where everyone gathered in the morning, at noon, and again in the evening. She enjoyed having a hand in the food preparation. The meals were plentiful but very plain. Meat—beef, pork, or wild game such as deer or elk—potatoes and vegetables at every meal. They served almost no fish. A hearty bread pudding or heavy cake usually completed each meal. Each passing day Betsy alarmingly felt her corset tightening a teeny bit more. She was not accustomed to such a heavy diet.

Unlike her English employment experience, table manners were basically unheard of in this home. It seemed to Betsy that the point of their mealtime was to eat as much as possible in the shortest amount of time. This was so unlike the refined, drawn-out mealtimes at the Turnballs'. Nobody dressed up for meals and the table settings were about as practical as one could imagine. But in their favour, the Browns insisted she join them at the table for meals, thereby making her feel much more like a regular member of the family.

Betsy had been given a small room on the main floor at the back of the house, with a window that overlooked a large field of newly planted wheat. She found that she loved to sleep with the window open, allowing the sweet, fresh prairie air to waft into the room. She was still not used to the howling of the wolves or the baying of the coyotes during the night. The prairie rain, too, was so different from that back home in England. Here it pelted down in sheets, quickly flooding the roads. This was in contrast to the light, misty rains of her Derbyshire homeland.

She and the black puppy became fast friends. She named him Watson because of his sleuth-like personality that reminded her of Sherlock Holmes' Watson, and of her father, Watty. Watson followed her about the farm as she did her chores and at night he snuggled up in bed with her. She was most grateful to George for his kindness and sensitivity in recognizing the value of having a pet to ease feelings of loneliness and homesickness. She was grateful to George for always making a point of including her in the lively dinner conversations held at the evening meal. *He really is a dear,* she thought.

CHAPTER SIXTEEN:
REVELATIONS

June 15, 1912

Betsy wasn't sure when the signs finally began to make sense. Later, she was amazed that she hadn't connected the dots sooner. In all of the rushing and planning to prepare for the trip, and the motion sickness she endured on the passage, she had lost track of when her monthlies should have come. The growing tightness of her corset, a lack of menstrual periods, morning sickness, and a fullness in her breasts—the signs were all there.

The dilemma for her now was what to do about it. When she stopped and counted the days she figured she must be about three and a half or four months along. She would be starting to show very soon, which would jeopardize her new employment. Mrs. Brown would surely not allow her to remain working on the farm alongside her five strictly raised boys and virginal daughter, Vera.

"What a fine mess I have created," she lamented to the hogs and sows as she poured slop into their trough. They were unhelpful, being totally focused on hungrily gobbling down the food scraps.

One thing was very clear from day one, that George, nearly eight years her junior, had taken a strong fancy to her. She eyed him now as he pulled down forkloads of hay for the horses in their stalls. She could see his firm muscles through his thin shirt. Sweat beaded on his broad forehead. She had been drawn from the start to his deep-set eyes and firm jaw. Standing six feet tall, he towered a foot over her whenever they stood near each other.

He grinned at her when he noticed her watching him. Usually it was the other way around, him watching her and admiring her soft curves and the way a strand of her long hair fell across her face when it came loose. He never tired of her sweet English accent and loved to hear her tell stories of her crossing over to Canada and, all those she had met en route. Of course, Mother was ever watchful. While he would have liked to ask Betsy to go walking down a country lane after dinner, he knew his mother would not approve. So he had resisted any urges to reveal his true feelings to Betsy. Until now.

"Hey little English Rose, how are you making out with those hogs?" he called out to her.

"Okay, I guess," she called back. "They sure do gobble up the slop. No wonder they're so plump and healthy. When do these ones get slaughtered?"

"Not until fall. They will be even fatter then. We'll be able to provide for ourselves and still have plenty to take to market from this lot." As Betsy was leaving the hog pen one of the large sows charged at her, trying to get at the feed bucket. George rushed over, clasping her in his arms preventing her fall. Holding Betsy closely, and firmly to his chest, George managed to close the gate saving her and preventing the hog's escape.

They remained in each other's arms then George bent his six-foot frame down and kissed Betsy passionately on her lips. Both were covered in dust and sweat from their labours, but neither seemed to notice. Swallows could be heard whooshing in and out of the hayloft and the pungent odours of hay, manure, and hog feed permeated the air.

George finally could not contain himself. Facing her, he announced in a low, soft voice, "Miss Betsy, I have a confession to make."

Betsy lowered her eyelids. "And what might that be?" she demurely inquired. As if she did not already have a clue. *He's struggling to find the right words,* she thought, watching him. *That's so sweet.* "Go on," she said aloud.

He licked his lips. He wiped his hands on his trousers. "Ever since you arrived here, a few short weeks ago, I have been unable to think about much else. I don't know what you did to me, but you are the first thing I think of when I wake, and at night I can barely sleep at night for thoughts of you. You are different from any girl I have met around here. You have sophistication about you. Even though you are out here in the barn helping with the chores, you seem so refined, so proper, so good." He paused and cleared his throat.

He paused, out of breath. Had he gone too far? Would she be alarmed and withdraw from his advances? Had he ruined everything? He was amazed to realize his knees were weak. *If she doesn't say something quickly, I may collapse right here on the barn floor.*

"Oh George," Betsy said "I also think of you first thing when I awake. You are the kindest, sweetest most honest man I have ever met. I admit to having fantasies about well...a future together with you."

She hesitated. Betsy realized that her secret was not going to remain hidden in the very near future.. *Is this the time to tell George about the baby? Will that change his mind completely about wanting to marry me? Will he think me a loose woman? And whatever will his mother say? It's bad enough that I'm eight years his senior, let alone pregnant with another man's child. It would be better to know now if he will withdraw from me, knowing my dark past.*

She drew a deep breath. "George, I have something to tell you before we go on. Before I left England I had a love affair with a very dear man—"

George interrupted her. "Betsy, I won't ask about anything in your past. You came here to start a new life. Nothing you did before would have any impact on the possibility of our future together. You are so beautiful, I would fully expect that you have had other men interested in you before now. For the life of me I can't imagine why none of them were able to secure your hand in marriage. Not that I'm complaining, mind you," he added quickly, with a self-conscious chuckle. "By Jove, if you had married one of them you wouldn't be here today, and I would have never found you."

Betsy braced herself before saying, "But there is more, George. And it would affect you and our lives together. I have found myself to be in a family way. I am nearly four months along and it will be starting to become obvious very soon now. The father never knew of the pregnancy; nor did I, until recently. I won't blame you if you change your feelings about me and want to end this right here and now. You would have every right."

George hesitated for but a moment. It was only to be sure that he could come up with the right words. "Oh, Betsy. This doesn't change a bit how I feel about you. In fact, it just makes me feel even more protective of you. I want to provide a good home for you and the little one. It's not the baby's fault; he didn't ask to be born. And you are going to need a strong shoulder to lean on. No, if anything, I love you more."

Tears welled up in Betsy's eyes. How could she be so lucky, to have found love in this godforsaken place and in the condition she was in? She didn't know, but she was grateful. They sat hand in hand on a bale of hay, plotting out how and when they'd break the news to Mrs. Brown and the others. It would not be easy. "There will be a scene, George warned. "But I'm an adult, and free to make my own choices."

Betsy was reminded of her conversations with Rosa concerning men who could not stand up to their mothers. *Thank you, God, for sending me one with a backbone,* she silently prayed.

* * *

RR 6, Section 12
Tregarva, Saskatchewan
Canada
June 5, 1912

My Dearest Father,

Your most welcome letter of May 1, 1912 was received safely today. I hope that by now you will have recovered from your illness and are feeling better. I so enjoyed hearing from you and appreciated your detailed accounts of all the neighbourhood comings and goings.

When our ship arrived in New York it was a lovely, bright morning. The sea was like a mill pond and as green as grass. We had two tugs to pull us to the dock and there was some delay in getting off the ship; we were not allowed to disembark until after dinner. But once we were off, they located our luggage quite quickly and I even had a hand in getting it to the train we boarded to Canada.

As soon as we disembarked, those of us bound for Canada were shown up a broad stairway on the southern side of the building. Turning to the left, we passed through ten aisles, where were stationed as many registry clerks. After being registered, those of the immigrants who had to be detained were placed in a wire-screened enclosure. The more fortunate ones of us passed on to a similar compartment.

All we had to do was show the immigration officer the landing card that we were given by the medical officer on board the ship. He asked the details of where we were heading, how much money we had, whether we had work, etc. It was interesting that first and second class passengers who arrived were not required to undergo a detailed inspection process at Ellis Island. Instead, we passengers underwent a cursory inspection aboard ship, the theory being that if a person could afford to purchase a first or second class ticket, they were less likely to end up in institutions or hospitals in America or become a burden to the state. However, some of the first and second class passengers were sent on for further inspection if they were sick or had legal problems.

There was an information bureau in the building for the benefit of those seeking friends or relatives among the immigrants. There were also telegraph and railroad ticket offices and a moneychanger's office. From there I purchased my train ticket and, with assistance from a fellow traveller, made my way to the train station. The train ride was uneventful, although I was very tired and not fully recovered from the voyage. I will tell you more about the trip over in a separate letter. It certainly was *an adventure. I am writing it all out in the form of a diary of sorts.*

Well Father, I have begun to settle into my new life here on the Prairies of Saskatchewan. It is unlike anything I imagined, though. The countryside is flat and bleak with none of the trees, mountains, and rivers that we saw in the slide show back home. It has its own beauty though, and the sunsets are something to behold. The whole sky lights up first in tones of pink and blue, then gradually turning almost violet and purple. The black night creeps up like fingers over the horizon. I never tire of watching this incredible display of beauty. And stars. My God, what a show they make from one end of the horizon to the other!

The family that I have employment with are most interesting. They consist of Mrs. Brown, her five sons, and one daughter named Vera. The master died in a farming accident several years ago. Mrs. Brown runs a seeding outfit here with her sons. They plant most of the fields in the surrounding area. She is a tough slave master, and works hard at keeping the boys in line at all times. She doesn't quite know how to take me, though. I think she is surprised that I am not afraid to get my hands dirty and work in the garden, the barn, or even the fields if that is what is needed.

One of the boys, George, is particularly handsome. He was the one sent to pick me up at the station when I arrived here. He has taken me aside on several occasions to warn me about things that annoy his mother. For example, I was always taught to steep the tea for five minutes before pouring the first cup. She insists on having her tea very weak, only letting it sit a minute or so. I suspect she may reuse the tealeaves several times. But then again, provisions are somewhat scarce here and she may just be being frugal. For example, Vera only got a new dress as a child when the flour ran out. The sack was dyed and used to create the new frock. We were lucky back home that we were never quite this poor, although I am sure Mama had many little cost-cutting practices that we never knew of.

Regarding young George, it is becoming clear that his interest in me is more than platonic. Although he is only eighteen, he seems very mature for his age. He knows everything about farming. He is six feet tall, has broad shoulders, and his hands are large and already gnarled. He has asked me my age, which I am reluctant to divulge, as you can well imagine. I usually just give my typical response: "I am as old as my tongue and a little bit older than my teeth." I don't feel that our age difference should be a barrier to our relationship.

He told me that, should we decide to marry—and in fact we already have discussed this—his mother might consent to having us live in one of the granaries in the back forty. Imagine. Me in a freestanding home of my own. I know it wouldn't be very elegant, but given the bleak chances for social advancement in England, it would feel like a castle. I will keep you posted of developments in this regard.

Well, Father, you will be tired from reading through all the foregoing, but I wanted to tell you of my safe arrival and let you know how much I love you and miss you. I have not had time to do much tatting on my lace collars and cuffs.

Besides, the women here tend to dress much more plainly than at home, so I don't know if there would be much of a market for them. Perhaps I will become a specialist in designing flour sack dresses. (Smile)

Much love to you,

Your Betsy

CHAPTER SEVENTEEN:
A FRESH BEGINNING

June 17, 1912

George thought long and hard about how best to break the news to his mother. He chose to do it on a Sunday. It was the one day of the week that she seemed a little more at peace with the world, especially after attending church and serving up a sumptuous meal of roast beef and all the trimmings. He waited until the washing up was complete, then asked if he might have a word alone with her.

Mother Brown removed her apron and brought a cup of tea with her into the formal living room, a space not often used during the week. She sank down on the soft, dark maroon sofa and gave a weary sigh.

"You look tired, Mother," commented George.

"Yes, I am, son. It just seems that the work is never done here. We get everything caught up on Saturday and by Monday it's time to start all over again. I don't know how I would manage without you boys here to do all the hard labour."

George nodded. "Well, if it's any consolation, we should realize an excellent return on our seeding efforts. The locust plague that everyone predicted seems to have evaded us here and we have had several good rains since the crops went in. I don't mind working hard if it pays off in the end."

"Yes, that is good news, son. But we shouldn't count our chickens too soon. I remember one year, when your father and I first came here, that our crops got completely wiped out in August when we had a severe hailstorm. You can't be sure of anything as a farmer."

Several moments of silence ensued. Surely Mother Brown could see her son was anxious, but she did nothing to lessen the tension. Perhaps she sensed what was coming.

Finally George spoke. "Mother, I have made a decision and I would like to seek your blessing. This will come as a shock perhaps, but I have grown very fond of Miss Betsy, our hired hand. In fact, we have declared our love for each other, and she has agreed to be my wife. Under the circumstances, I see no reason why we should put off matrimony."

Mary Anne turned white. She'd been anticipating a request to begin the process of courting the young lady, as she had seen the looks they had been exchanging and noticed her son paying attention to his hair, his clothes, and his personal hygiene. These were the telltale signs of a young man falling in love. But *this* was unheard of—marriage within barely a month of meeting the young lady! What would everyone in the district say? How would she hold her head up? She must put a halt to this impulsive behaviour at once.

"George, George, George," she began, "of course you are moonstruck by this young woman. She has obviously plied her charms on you, and perhaps you have done the same to her. But the idea of marrying so soon is out of the question. You have barely known each other for a month, hardly time to really know one another at all. Such a hasty marriage would surely be doomed to failure. I can't in all conscience allow this. Your father would not approve either, were he here to consult on the matter."

George looked down but not downcast. "Mother, at this point, my marriage to Betsy is not up for discussion. I came to seek your blessing, not your permission."

Another several moments of silence. Then George spoke again. "Mother, I think I should be honest and tell you now that there is another reason Betsy and I wish to marry immediately. Betsy left a man in England with whom she was involved for some time. She has unexpectedly found herself in a family way. I have told her that that does not change my feelings for her and I want to raise the child as if he or she were my own. Tongues will wag when people do the math, but we don't care."

"Oh George, how can you do this to me? To our family? The nerve of her, asking you to take on another man's child! Why, I can't believe my ears. She must be at least ten years older than you, as well." Mary Anne's shock rapidly turned to anger, and she braced her hands on the arms of her chair and half rose. "How could you have fallen for such a scam? Have I taught you nothing? I will tell you one thing—I never want to see that hussy grace my doorstep again."

George quietly stood. "Mother, I can see you are upset. I am sorry to cause you such angst. We have set the date for our wedding to be in two weeks. Betsy is sewing her wedding dress now, and I have asked Will Seed and Vera to stand up for us. Betsy is sewing Vera's dress, as well. The wedding will take place in Regina City Hall. I'll talk with you tomorrow about where we might live afterwards. I was hoping we might be able to fix up one of the granaries to use in the short run. But we have time to deal with these issues. I will leave you now and say good night."

Mrs. Brown put her hands over her face and began to sob as George backed out of the room.

George had figured his mother would be upset, but he'd not counted on her being quite so angry. *Perhaps in a day or two she will calm down and come to her senses,* he thought as he headed to his bedroom. He dreaded having to tell Betsy about his mother's reaction, but decided he had better do so before turning in. As he passed her room he saw that the light was on, so he knocked on her door. She opened it and invited him to come in.

George gently closed the door and turned and embraced Betsy warmly. He had never felt so protective in his life and swore under his breath that he would never let any harm come to his dear little bride-to-be.

The puppy, Watson, clamoured around his feet for attention, so he bent down and scratched his ears.

"How did it go, my love?" Betsy asked anxiously.

"Rather about what I expected," George sighed. He straightened. "Perhaps a little worse. She was doing not too badly with the idea of us courting; had we given her more time, I think she might have even come to accept the idea of our marriage. However, when I told her about the baby, she was very upset."

Worry pinched Betsy's eyebrows together. "Does this mean we should put off the plans for the wedding in two weeks?"

"Absolutely not," George replied adamantly. "It will go ahead as scheduled. I am longing for the moment I can call you my wife."

That night, Betsy had difficulty falling asleep. She felt so good about marrying dear George, but hated the fact that he had to endure his mother's harsh anger. How would her father react when she broke the news? She did not want to let him down or bring unnecessary shame to her family. She made a decision that she would tell him of the wedding but forestall news of the baby until later. He would never know the difference, being so far away.

* * *

The following day, Mrs. Brown asked to speak to Betsy in private. The two women moved into the living room.

Mrs. Brown immediately turned and confronted Betsy. "Why have you done this to my son, young lady? You really have a nerve, hoodwinking him into marriage, and then demanding that he raise another man's child as his own. He is merely 18 and you, how old are you? Who is this baby's father, and why doesn't he bear the responsibility of raising his own child?"

Betsy faced Mrs. Brown squarely and looked directly into her eyes. "Mrs. Brown, I am so sorry to have caused you this pain. It was never my intention to hurt you. You have been so kind to me. And falling in love with your son was the last thing I planned. The fact that I am carrying a baby conceived with someone else is not an issue for George. He will be the child's father in all of the ways that matter. I hope one day you will be our baby's grandmother. And as for my age, I am only a few years older than George."

Mrs. Brown threw up her hands, but when she spoke her voice, though hard, was no longer shrill. "Well, I can see you have both made up your minds. I don't approve and never will. You can make up the granary in the south pasture as living quarters for you and George to occupy once you are married. I will expect you to sleep and eat there and to only come to the house to assist in your duties as a farm hand. You will have to share the family outhouse for the time being, but I demand that George build a new one before the summer is over. That's all. I must get on with the chores." She pushed past Betsy and left the room.

Betsy stood alone for a few minutes. Mrs. Brown's wrath aside, she pondered how a nasty situation could have turned out to be such a wonderful thing. Once more in her life, an apparent tragedy has been turned into an exciting new opportunity. Hard work and hard times lay ahead, but she felt that she had strength to face it all. The mother-in-law...well that would take some time. The Swadlincote town clock flashed before her eyes..."Time the Avenger". Maybe there was hope that one day she would truly be welcomed into this family.

* * *

March 15, 1915

Betsy was still busy unpacking to settle into the small farmhouse she now occupied with George, Kenneth who by now was 2, and her newest baby Margery. It had been a particularly cold winter and the snow had barely begun to show signs of melting in the fields. She tossed another log onto the fireplace and began planning the evening meal while putting away the last of the pots and pans.

The door opened and George lumbered in, his tall lanky frame filling the entranceway. He'd brought a few supplies from town, including a sac of flour. Betsy was pleased. The flour sac would be turned into a fine pair of jumpers for Kenneth and a few wee dresses for Margery. Nothing would be wasted. The apples he brought were welcomed too, each wrapped in its own little blanket of tissue paper. The papers would be collected, folded, and placed in the outhouse in place of toilet paper.

That was when she saw it, the letter that had come in the mail. Immediately Betsy recognized the handwriting to be that of her dear travel companion on the Olympic – Rosa. They had kept in touch by mail ever since the crossing and even had talked about plans to have Rosa come for a visit when next she had a long vacation.

Betsy wiped her hands on her apron and went to sit by the fire. She carefully opened the envelope and slipped out the letter. Excitement mounted as she prepared to revel in her friends accounts of wonderful adventures abroad and in America. But her heart sank as she began reading.

March 1, 1915

Dearest Betsy:

It is with a heavy heart that I write to give you some sad news. I have been afflicted with an incurable illness and the doctors here in England tell me I have only months to live. I wish with all my heart that it wasn't so but I do take some comfort in knowing I will once again be united with Harold, the only man I have ever truly loved.

I want to wish you all the best in your new life on the Canadian prairies and hope that that handsome husband treats you well. Maybe his mother will even come around one day and accept you into the family.

This will in all probability be my last letter to you. Be brave. I have treasured our friendship so much. Ciao belle.

Rosa

In shock, Betsy sat staring at the paper in her hand. She took the envelope and was about to toss it into the fireplace when a small silver object slipped out and fell onto the hearth. Reaching down she realized what it was and grasping the wee silver heart in her hand, she wept.

Betsy, George, Will and Vera.

George, Betsy and the first 3 of their 4 children.

LIST OF REFERENCES AND SOURCES CONSULTED

References

1. "The National Archives Learning Curve | Britain 1906-18 | Achievements of Liberal Welfare Reforms: Gallery . Learningcurve.gov.uk.

2. boards.ancestry.ca > Surnames > Snape. "John William Snape (34) showman, charged with having permitted, or suffered to be acted, in a certain place, to wit a booth in Derby St., a certain stage play "Little Bo Peep", the said place not being a patent theatre under the statute on that behalf. Fined 2s 6d and 19s 6d costs."

3. The Burton Observer, Thursday, April 18, 1912.

4. *The Last Dinner on the Titanic*, p.139

5. Nutt, Graham. *Stranger, a Ghost and a Conjuror: Three Stories Based on True Events in South Derbyshire*. 1996

6. www.pacinst.com/terrorists/ chapter5/titanic.html.

Internet Sources

http://www.bbc.co.uk/southampton/ features/titanic/onboard1.shtml

http://www.boards.ancestry.ca

http://www.encyclopedia-titanica.org/ canceled-titanic-passages.html

http://www.encyclopedia-titanica. org/**violet-jessop**-vad.html

http://www.Learningcurve.gov.uk.

http://www.lva.virginia.gov/exhib-its/titanic/titanic1.htm#tlist

http://members.aol.com/WakkoW5/Plympic.html

http://www.pacinst.com/terror-ists/chapter5/titanic.html

http://www.spartacus.school-net.co.uk/PRasquith.htm

http://www.spartacus.schoolnet.co.uk/Lold.htm

http://www.thehistorybox.com/ny_city/society/
printerfriendly/nycity_society_english_manners

http://www.titanicinquiry.org/ships/oceanic.php

http://titanic-whitestarships.com/MGY_Jessop.htm

http://www.titanic-titanic.com/after-
math_of_titanic_sinking.shtml

http://titanicandco.com/inside.html

http://en.wikipedia.org/wiki/
Titanic_alternative_theories

http://www.writing.eng.vt.edu/uer/bassett.html

Book and Journal Sources

Ballard, Robert. (1987). The Discovery of the
Titanic. Madison Press Books, Toronto.

Hyslop, Donald, Forsyth, Alastair and
Jemima, Sheila. (1994). Titanic Voices. Sutton
Publishing Limited, Thrupp, Gloucestershire.

Jessop, Violet (1997). Titanic Survivor.
Sheridan House Inc., Dobbs Ferry, NY.

Nutt, Graham. (1996). A Stranger, a Ghost and a
Conjuror. Avenger Publications, Swadlincote.

Nutt, Graham. (1992). Tuppenny Rush. Trent
Valley Publications, Burton-on-Trent.

The Burton Observer, Thursday, April 18, 1912

Wouters, Cas. Etiquette Books and Emotion Management in the 20th Century: Part One: The Integration of Social Class. Journal of Social History, Vol 29, No 1 (Autumn, 1995), pp. 107-124.